❤ ❤ ❤

Joe planned to distance himself from Brynn, to decide what it was about her that kept her on his mind.

So as he approached his brother's home, he told himself it was simply to visit his family and make sure all was going well with Brynn as the new nanny. After all, he felt responsible for her being there. He'd asked his huge, boisterous family to watch out for Brynn after her accident.

But when Joe entered the house, all his careful planning fell apart.

Brynn stood there, cradling his infant nephew in her arms, cooing to him with a look of utter infatuation on her face.

Joe's tongue went numb. He couldn't have spoken if he'd tried.

Suddenly Brynn looked up; her eyes met Joe's, then widened.

And something very special arced between them. Something neither could deny....

Dear Reader,

This month, Silhouette Special Edition presents an exciting selection of stories about forever love, fanciful weddings—and the warm bonds of family.

Longtime author Gina Wilkins returns to Special Edition with *Her Very Own Family,* which is part of her FAMILY FOUND: SONS & DAUGHTERS series. The Walker and D'Alessandro clans first captivated readers when they were introduced in the author's original Special Edition series, FAMILY FOUND. In this new story, THAT SPECIAL WOMAN! Brynn Larkin's life is about to change when she finds herself being wooed by a drop-dead gorgeous surgeon....

The heroines in these next three books are destined for happiness—or are they? First, Susan Mallery concludes her enchanting series duet, BRIDES OF BRADLEY HOUSE, with a story about a hometown nanny who becomes infatuated with her very own *Dream Groom.* Then the rocky road to love continues with *The Long Way Home* by RITA Award-winning author Cheryl Reavis—a poignant tale about a street-smart gal who finds acceptance where she least expects it. And you won't want to miss the passionate reunion romance in *If I Only Had a... Husband* by Andrea Edwards. This book launches the fun-filled new series, THE BRIDAL CIRCLE, about four long-term friends who discover there's no place like home—to find romance!

Rounding off the month, we have *Accidental Parents* by Jane Toombs—an emotional story about an orphan who draws his new parents together. And a no-strings-attached arrangement goes awry when a newlywed couple becomes truly smitten in *Their Marriage Contract* by Val Daniels.

I hope you enjoy all our selections this month!

Sincerely,

Karen Taylor Richman
Senior Editor

Please address questions and book requests to:
Silhouette Reader Service
U.S.: 3010 Walden Ave., P.O. Box 1325, Buffalo, NY 14269
Canadian: P.O. Box 609, Fort Erie, Ont. L2A 5X3

GINA WILKINS
HER VERY OWN FAMILY

Silhouette®

SPECIAL EDITION®

Published by Silhouette Books

America's Publisher of Contemporary Romance

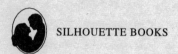 SILHOUETTE BOOKS

ISBN 0-373-24243-3

HER VERY OWN FAMILY

Look us up on-line at: http://www.romance.net

Printed in U.S.A.

GINA WILKINS

declares that she is Southern by birth and by choice, and she has chosen to set many of her books in the South, where she finds a rich treasury of characters and settings. She particularly loves the Ozark mountain region of northern Arkansas and southern Missouri, and the proudly unique people who reside there. She and her husband, John, live in Arkansas with their three children, Courtney, Kerry and David.

Dear Reader,

Several years ago, I wrote the FAMILY FOUND series about siblings separated as small children who find each other again as adults—and discover romance during the journey. I fell hard for the Walker and D'Alessandro families, and I have wanted to visit them again ever since. It always pleased me when readers wrote to make the same request. I'd left behind the younger son of the D'Alessandro family, and I've always known that Joe would someday want a romance of his own. But I knew it would take a very special woman to suit this dashing doctor....

When Brynn Larkin's personality began to form in my mind, I knew I'd found someone who desperately needed a family of her own. Her unsettled childhood has left her wondering if she can ever known belong to a family, though it is something she has always dreamed of. She literally crashes into Dr. Joe D'Alessandro's path—and neither his life nor hers will ever be the same.

For those who are familiar with the FAMILY FOUND series, I hope you enjoy revisiting them as much as I have. And for those who have yet to be introduced to the Walker and D'Alessandro clans, I hope they become as special to you as they are to me. I will be visiting them again with *That First Special Kiss*—coming to Silhouette Special Edition in September 1999!

Gina Wilkins

Chapter One

Dr. Joe D'Alessandro had been at the hospital for hours. He was tired and hungry, eager to get home after a long, eventful day that had begun, for him, at 5 a.m. It was after 6 p.m. now, and he hadn't even had a chance to eat lunch. But when a speeding pickup truck entered the highway, going the wrong way on an exit ramp, and rammed into the passenger side of a compact car just ahead of Joe's vehicle, he never even considered driving on, leaving someone else to deal with the mess. Almost before the sound of the horrendous crash had completely faded, Joe was out of his car and running to help.

His brother Michael, who'd been riding with Joe home from the hospital where they'd just welcomed a new addition to the D'Alessandro family, was close on Joe's heels. "I'll check the truck," he shouted. "You look after the other car."

Joe nodded and sprinted toward the driver's side of
the car that had taken the impact. The older model, pre-
airbag car, had been built more for economy than safety.
The passenger door was crushed against the front of the
truck. Joe hoped no one had been riding in the passenger seat, but it took only a glance inside the vehicle to
see that both front seats were occupied.

Two young women were in the car, and they were
both ominously still. Boxes and suitcases were tumbled
throughout the interior of the small, crumpled vehicle,
taking even more of the available space.

Other people were beginning to gather, shouting
questions and suggestions.

"I called 911. Should we try to get them out of the
car?" a burly, breathless young man asked Joe as he
joined him beside the car door.

"Not yet." Joe opened the driver's door of the compact and knelt inside to check the driver. "I'm a doctor," he said over his shoulder. "Unless there's someone else with medical training out there, have everyone
stand back out of the way."

The young man took Joe's words seriously, turning
immediately to hold out his arms and motion the gathering onlookers off. "Stand back, everyone," he
shouted. "We've got a doctor here."

The car's driver moaned when Joe pressed his fingers
to her neck to check her pulse. Her eyes fluttered,
opened, then squinted in the yellow glare of the interior
lighting. She was young, Joe noted objectively. Pretty.
And terrified when she came to full consciousness and
realized what had happened.

Gasping, she surged forward, would have toppled
right out of the car if her seat belt hadn't restrained her.

Joe caught her shoulders, steadying her. "It's all right," he said firmly. "I'm a doctor. I'm here to help you."

"What...?"

She blinked, looking confused. Joe didn't think she'd been knocked unconscious, but she was badly shaken.

"Can you tell me your name?"

"Brynn Larkin. I..." Lifting a hand to her head, she frowned, then jerked around to look at her passenger. Her gasp was anguished. *"Kelly!"*

"Help is on the way," Joe promised, reaching out to take her shoulders. "I'm a doctor," he repeated firmly, when he saw panic begin to suffuse her face. "Are you in pain?"

Still looking at the other woman, Brynn shook her head. "I'm fine. Please, help my friend. She's hurt."

"I can't get to her," Joe said. "The truck that hit you is completely blocking the other side of your car."

Brynn fumbled desperately for the latch of her seat belt. She winced with the movements, showing discomfort but no evidence of serious injuries. A swelling lump on her temple was the only damage Joe could see, probably from where the side of her head had hit the driver's window. She seemed coherent enough; he thought she'd be all right. Her friend, however, was a different matter. Even from where he knelt, Joe could tell that the other woman had not been as fortunate.

He took Brynn's arm, steadying her as she slid out from behind the wheel to give him better access to her friend. "Please help her," she begged.

Michael appeared at Joe's side. "Lean on me, ma'am," he said, taking the driver's arm as she rose shakily to her feet. "My brother will see what he can do for your friend while you and I wait right here for the ambulance."

She refused to move more than a step from the open car door. Joe slid quickly into the seat she'd vacated. A big, leather purse was in his way; he scooped it up and tossed it backward, aware that Brynn caught it and clutched it in her arms. A glance over his shoulder told Joe that Michael was hovering protectively beside her, and then Joe turned his attention to the more seriously injured young woman.

Her head was slumped over the seat belt, which now rested across her throat. Very carefully, Joe moved her head to ease the pressure on her airway. Mentally cursing the fading daylight, he rapidly assessed her visible injuries.

There were too many of them.

The driver leaned into the doorway behind him, her voice frantic. "Is she breathing? Please, how is she?"

Hearing imminent hysteria, Joe spoke soothingly over his shoulder, the majority of his attention still focused on the injured woman. "She's breathing. I'm taking care of her, Brynn. Stand back, now, so the emergency teams can get to us."

Already the sound of approaching sirens was growing louder, to Joe's relief. Kelly needed help, and quickly, but there was little he could do as long as she was all but enfolded in the buckled metal of the car. "Michael?"

"Yes?"

Joe glanced through the jagged-edged opening of the broken passenger window toward the smashed truck. "Is someone taking care of the other driver?"

"He's all right. Drunk as a skunk, but he's sobering fast. I've got a few guys keeping an eye on him until the police get here." Michael's tone held pure disgust when he talked about the negligent driver.

Joe grimaced and returned his full concentration to the unconscious woman in front of him. If it were up to him, he thought, the drunk would pay dearly for what he'd done to this young woman.

Brynn's head hurt, but she ignored the pain, her full concentration centered in that horribly mangled car with Kelly. She was dimly aware of the man who stood so close to her side, his hand resting supportively on her shoulder, but she didn't bother to look at him. She was more concerned with the man in the car with Kelly, the one who'd identified himself as a doctor.

Let him help her. Please.

Something about him reassured her, gave her hope. Maybe it was his deep, calm voice, or the kindness she'd seen in his brown eyes when he'd leaned over her and asked if she was in pain.

An ambulance pulled up among the people who had stopped to help or gawk. A patrol car arrived almost simultaneously, and an officer jumped out to send the onlookers away and clear access for emergency crews. Two EMTs rushed to the interlocked vehicles.

The man with Brynn stepped forward to brief the medics. ''This woman was driving the car that took the impact. Her friend is trapped inside. The man in the car with her is my brother, Dr. Joe D'Alessandro.''

The medics nodded and went to work. Brynn could hear Joe D'Alessandro updating them on Kelly's condition in frightening terms she couldn't understand and then barking orders which the EMTs efficiently followed.

Another ambulance pulled in behind the first. A tall, coffee-skinned woman in a crisp white uniform shirt with dark uniform slacks stepped in front of Brynn. "You were driving this car?"

Brynn nodded, feeling unspecified guilt flood through her. She had been driving the car. So why was she standing here now, relatively uninjured, while Kelly was…?

She swallowed painfully, feeling the threat of tears burn behind her eyes.

The medic brushed Brynn's hair away from the lump at her left temple. "I'm Gail. What's your name?"

"Brynn Larkin," Brynn answered mechanically.

"Come with me, Ms. Larkin, and let me have a look at you. And there's a very nice police officer who wants to take a statement from you about the accident."

"My friend…"

"Your friend is being cared for by professionals." Gail took Brynn's arm in a firm, yet gentle grip. "Let's get out of the way and let them work, shall we?"

Tears trickled down Brynn's cheeks. Clutching her purse, she nodded and allowed the woman to lead her to one of the waiting ambulances.

It took almost an hour for Kelly to be extricated from the wreckage. She regained consciousness soon after the ambulance teams arrived. Pain and fear made her words nearly incoherent, though she repeatedly said Brynn's name. Joe stayed with her the entire time, holding her hand, calling her by name, repeating that he was a doctor, reassuring her that Brynn was fine and that Kelly herself would receive the very best of care.

"Don't leave me," Kelly begged, clinging weakly to his hand and sobbing.

"I won't leave you," he promised. "You're going to be fine, Kelly."

He hoped he was telling her the truth.

It was an enormous relief to everyone when Kelly was finally lifted gently out of the wreckage and strapped to a waiting gurney.

Brynn had refused to be transported to the hospital until she knew her friend was out of the car. She rushed to the gurney, stumbling a little when she reached it.

Joe steadied her, then kept his hands on her shoulders, since her pale skin and wild eyes worried him. She hardly seemed to notice he was there. Her eyes were fixed on Kelly's bloody, mangled legs. The blood gushing from her right arm. The blood on her face.

"Kelly?" Brynn's voice was little more than a choked whisper.

Kelly moaned and groped weakly for her friend's hand. "Brynn. I hurt so bad."

A sob broke from Brynn's throat. "I know, sweetie," she murmured the words, barely audible. "I'm so sorry."

"We need to load her into the ambulance, ma'am," one of the medics said, his voice quietly sympathetic.

Joe pulled Brynn gently back from the gurney. "Let them get her to the hospital, Brynn. It would be best if you followed in the other ambulance. You'll only be a minute or two behind her, all right?"

She turned her tear-streaked face toward him, as though noticing for the first time how closely he stood to her. "Please," she said. "Ride with her, Dr. D'Alessandro. Take care of her."

Unexpectedly shaken by the appeal, and the blind faith it implied, Joe nodded. "I will. Michael..."

His brother stepped quickly forward. "I'll wait here until the cars are towed away. And then I'll join you at the hospital."

Joe nodded. "Thanks. Take Brynn to the other ambulance first, will you?"

Michael nodded. "Anything you want to get out of your car before you go, Ms. Larkin?"

Joe thought he'd never seen a more vulnerable expression than the one Brynn turned toward Michael. "Everything I own is in that car," she said simply, clinging even more tightly to the purse in her arms.

Michael glanced at Joe, then spoke to Brynn. "I'll take care of everything here," he said kindly. "You just worry about your friend and yourself right now."

"Thank you," she whispered.

Joe touched his brother's arm in gratitude before climbing into the ambulance behind Kelly's gurney.

By the time the ambulance arrived at the hospital where Joe had already spent most of the day, he had examined Kelly as thoroughly as possible under the circumstances, and knew what would have to be done for her. After sending Kelly off with the emergency team to be prepped, he was waiting when Brynn was wheeled into the ER futilely insisting that she did *not* need a wheelchair and that she wanted to see her friend.

Joe got his first real look at her then, under the harsh lights of the hospital emergency entrance. Bruised, pale and shaken, she was still a very attractive woman, probably somewhere in her mid-twenties. Her tousled nape-length, blunt-cut hair was almost as dark as his own, but her eyes were a clear, crystalline blue. The unexpected contrast was very appealing, particularly in combination with her delicately rounded face, small, straight nose and full, soft mouth.

She spotted him and climbed quickly out of the

wheelchair, resisting a nurse's attempts to keep her seated.

"Dr. D'Alessandro," Brynn said urgently. "Where is Kelly? What's being done for her? When can I see her?"

"Your friend is being stabilized and prepped for surgery," Joe answered in the soothing voice he typically used for hysterical family members.

"Surgery?" Brynn whispered.

He nodded. "She has sustained a rather serious injury to her right leg, as you saw at the accident scene. There are other injuries, as well, but her leg took the brunt of the damage. I'm an orthopedic surgeon on staff here, so I will perform the operation, if you have no objection."

She moistened her colorless lips, gripped her possessions more tightly in her arms and looked him in the eyes when she asked, "Are you good?"

"I'm good," he answered simply—because it was what she needed to hear, and because it was true.

"He's the best, ma'am," the hovering nurse piped in.

Joe sent her a slight smile of thanks, then looked back at Brynn. "You'll want to call your friend's family."

"She doesn't have a family. She and I were raised in the same foster home. I'm all the family she has—and she's all I have."

"Is there anyone else we can call for you, Ms. Larkin? A friend, perhaps?" the nurse asked.

Brynn shook her head. "We're new to Dallas. We don't know anyone here yet."

Joe frowned, feeling the urge to hurry to his patient but hating to leave Brynn so alone. "I want you to be thoroughly examined, as well. You've been so worried about your friend that you haven't taken time to assess your own condition.''

"I'm fine," Brynn answered impatiently. "Kelly is the one who's hurt." She looked at him pleadingly. "Please go help her."

Joe placed a hand on her shoulder. She felt very fragile beneath his hand, as if she were holding herself together by sheer willpower. "I'll take care of her," he promised.

He turned then to the nurse. "Do me a favor, will you?" he asked quietly. "See if any D'Alessandros or Walkers are still hanging around in the maternity ward. Ms. Larkin needs someone with her."

The woman nodded and hurried away. Joe led Brynn to a vinyl-covered bench at an unoccupied end of the waiting room. He urged her to sit down and then sat beside her, explaining as simply and reassuringly as possible what the operation on her friend's leg would entail. By the time he'd finished, the nurse had returned, followed by a tough-looking, deeply tanned cowboy in flannel shirt, jeans and well-worn boots.

"Jared." Joe stood to greet the older man, pleased to see him. Jared Walker, with his calm, quiet strength, was the kind of man a frightened young woman would instinctively trust.

Jared nodded. "Hey, Joe. I understand there's been an accident."

Speaking quickly and in a low voice, Joe explained the situation to Jared, who looked at the slender young woman sitting alone and lost on the bench in the bustling emergency room and nodded. "I'll sit with her."

Joe clapped a hand on Jared's shoulder. "Thanks. She needs the support."

"No problem. I'd want someone to do the same if it was my Molly in this situation."

He led Jared to Brynn, who was watching them questioningly. "Brynn Larkin, this is Jared Walker, a very good friend of mine. He's going to stay here with you for a while, okay?"

"Oh, that really isn't necessary." Brynn's protest was automatic, and held a touch of shyness as she looked quickly from Jared to Joe.

Jared gave her one of his rare smiles, and Joe could almost see Brynn warm to it—as most people did, from what Joe had observed during the more than ten years he'd known Jared Walker.

"No trouble at all, ma'am," Jared drawled, his tone pure, laid-back Texan. "Hospitals are bad enough without having to sit in them by yourself."

Reassured that Brynn was in good hands, Joe excused himself and rushed off to scrub for surgery.

Brynn watched Joe disappear and then turned to the kind-eyed cowboy who had seated himself beside her on the hard bench. "You know him well?"

"Joe?" Jared Walker nodded. "I've known him quite awhile now. My sister Michelle is married to his brother Tony which makes us family, in a manner of speaking."

Brynn thought of the man who'd assisted her at the scene of the accident, who had introduced himself as Joe's brother Michael. She wondered briefly how many brothers the doctor had, but she pushed that question aside to concentrate on one that was much more important at the moment.

"He's a good surgeon?"

Jared answered without hesitation. "I would let him operate on my wife, my son or my daughter. If you knew me better, you would understand how much confidence in him that indicates.''

Jared's love for his family was so obvious that Brynn's throat tightened in reaction. ''Thank you for reassuring me that Kelly's in good hands,'' she murmured.

''I can tell you're very close to your friend.''

''She's…'' Brynn had to clear her throat. ''She's like a sister to me. The only family I have. I don't know how I would bear it if…if she…''

Jared covered Brynn's icy, clenched fingers with his own work-hardened hand. ''Joe will do everything he can,'' he said.

She might have preferred a reckless promise that Kelly would be fine, that there was no chance Brynn would lose her. Somehow she knew Jared Walker wasn't the kind of man who made promises he wasn't so sure he could keep. She sighed and nodded, grateful for the comfort he'd offered. ''I know. It's just…I'm afraid.''

''I understand.''

Brynn bit her lip, doubting that he could possibly understand how she felt at this moment.

Jared's hand tightened around hers. ''I understand,'' he repeated. ''Eleven years ago, I sat in this very room waiting for word about my son, Shane, after a drunk driver ran a red light and smashed into the side of my truck. The side where my son was sitting.''

Brynn went very still, searching his face. She could almost see the grim memories mirrored in his dark-blue eyes.

''I had been driving,'' Jared added. ''I sat here, hardly injured, and blamed myself for the accident, even though there was nothing I could have done to prevent it. I thought if my son died, it would be my fault, because I should have seen the guy coming or reacted faster or something. It didn't seem fair that Shane was hurt so badly when I hardly had a scratch.''

Tears filled Brynn's eyes and spilled onto her cheeks. Jared Walker *did* understand how she felt. ''I never saw the other guy,'' she whispered, her voice quivering. ''He hit us before I even knew he was there. I couldn't do anything. I couldn't...''

Her breath caught.

''I know, Brynn,'' Jared murmured. ''I've been there. And it doesn't help to beat yourself up over something that wasn't your fault.''

''Your son...'' She wiped at her face with her free hand. ''He was all right?''

''He broke his arm. Bruised one leg. Within a couple of weeks he was playing tag with his cousins. He was fourteen then. He's twenty-five now. About your age, I would guess.''

She nodded. ''I'll be twenty-six in a few months.''

''How old is your friend?''

''Twenty-two.''

''So you're the 'big sister.' You feel responsible for her. Which is making you feel even more guilty about the accident.''

''I suppose so,'' she admitted, caught off-guard by his perceptiveness.

''Keep reminding yourself that it wasn't your fault. You'll start to believe it after a while.''

''I saw Kelly's right leg,'' Brynn murmured after a moment of silence. ''It's more than bruised. It was so bloody and twisted. She looked horrible.''

''Joe's an excellent orthopedic surgeon,'' Jared said

again. "He'll take care of her. You were fortunate that he was there when the accident happened."

"It's almost as if he was sent to be there for us," Brynn murmured.

"Maybe he was."

She wanted to believe that was true.

A uniformed hospital employee approached with a clipboard and a list of questions for Brynn. Jared sat patiently beside her as she answered as many as she could, trying to concentrate over the noise and activity going on around them. Once again, Brynn refused to be examined by a doctor; she insisted that she wanted to remain where she was until she had news of Kelly's condition.

"You're sure about this, Brynn?" Jared asked. "Car accident injuries can be sneaky."

"I'm fine," she repeated firmly. She was being truthful; other than feeling sore and stiff, she was uninjured. "How long do you suppose this operation will take?"

"It could take a long time," Jared warned. "If your friend's leg is as badly injured as you suspect, the repairs could take hours."

Brynn closed her eyes and shuddered, thinking again that Jared Walker was not a man prone to sugarcoating his answers. But he was being so kind to stay with her, a total stranger. She was certain he had other things to do.

She opened her eyes to look at him. "I'll be fine, you know, if you need to leave. I certainly can't expect you to wait here with me all evening."

He shrugged, looking perfectly content to remain where he was. "I've got nowhere else to be at the moment. I was here at the hospital because my sister had a baby this morning. My wife was here earlier, but

Molly—our ten-year-old daughter—had a mother-daughter thing at Girl Scouts this evening, so Cassie took her to that. Unless you would rather be alone, I would like to stay and keep you company. It's easier to wait when you have someone to talk to and take your mind off your worry.''

"I don't want to be alone," Brynn admitted. "Not if you really don't mind staying."

"I really don't mind." He sounded utterly sincere.

Brynn blinked back a fresh wave of tears, thinking that Joe D'Alessandro wasn't the only one who'd been heaven-sent to help her through this.

Half an hour into the operation, Brynn glanced up to see a good-looking man in boots, jeans and a denim shirt strolling toward the bench where she and Jared sat. He was of average height, athletically built, brown haired, tanned, and had gray-blue eyes so much like Jared Walker's that Brynn immediately guessed this must be Jared's son, Shane.

"Hi, Dad," he said, confirming her suspicion. "What's going on?"

Jared and Brynn both stood, and Jared made the introductions. Hearing what had happened, Shane looked sympathetically at Brynn. "Joe's an excellent surgeon. You couldn't ask for anyone better for your friend."

"So I've been told," Brynn murmured, glancing at Jared.

"Can I get you some coffee? A soda, maybe?" Shane offered, looking as though he would really like to do something to help.

Brynn started to decline, then realized that her mouth was very dry. "A soda sounds good," she said, a bit shyly. "If you don't mind…"

Shane was already in motion. "Be right back," he

promised. "I'll get you some coffee, Dad," he called over his shoulder.

Jared grimaced. "The coffee around here isn't much better than drinking lighter fluid. I should know—I've drunk enough of it."

Shane had hardly returned with the beverages when another man appeared, this one tall and handsome, with wavy dark hair, frosted with gray at the temples, and dark, smiling eyes.

Jared introduced him as Tony D'Alessandro, a name Brynn recognized.

"You're the new father," she said. "Congratulations."

Tony grinned. "Thank you. This is our fourth—and final—child."

"Boy or girl?"

"Boy. His name is Justin. We also have a nine-year-old boy, and two girls, ages six and four."

"A big family."

"My wife and I love children." Tony's smile faded. "I heard about what happened to you and your friend. Is there anything I can do to help you, Ms. Larkin?"

"'Brynn,'" she corrected him. "And thank you, but no, there's nothing you can do for now. I only wish I had some word about Kelly."

"Don't tell him I said so, but my brother is a heck of a surgeon," Tony assured her. "Your friend is getting the best of care."

Under any other circumstances, Brynn might have been somewhat amused by the repeated assurances that Joe D'Alessandro was such an excellent surgeon. Instead, she took each word to heart.

Brynn knew the time she spent waiting for word of Kelly's condition would have been pure hell had she been sitting there alone, bruised and sore and terrified. As it was, Jared, Shane and Tony kept her company, even making her smile several times with their banter. She wondered if she would ever be able to express the full extent of her gratitude to them.

Someone entered the waiting room and she glanced up expectantly, hoping for word of Kelly's progress. Instead, she recognized the new arrival as Michael D'Alessandro, from the accident scene. He was followed by an older man, who looked like a seventy-something version of the D'Alessandro brothers.

Michael walked straight to Brynn, nodding at the men surrounding her. "How are you?" he asked her.

"I'm fine. Kelly is in surgery. Your brother is operating on her leg."

Michael nodded, and Brynn was struck by how much he resembled his brother Tony. "Your car has been towed to a reputable body shop, though I imagine the insurance company will declare it a total loss. My father and I unloaded all your things from the car and took them to his house, where they'll be safe. We made an itemized list of everything, and we had a police officer watch what we removed and sign the list at the scene. We also gave the officer our names and Dad's address, in case you worried about our trustworthiness."

"Michael's a lawyer," Tony murmured with a smile for Brynn. "He believes in dotting every *i* and crossing every *t*."

"I don't know how to thank you," Brynn said to Michael, and then looked around the group to include the others. "All of you. You've been so kind to me."

The men cleared their throats, shuffled their feet and appeared embarrassed. And then all started talking at once, obviously wanting to change the subject.

Vinnie D'Alessandro sat beside Brynn, while the others scattered for a break. Tony and Michael went upstairs to check on the new baby; Jared and his son moved to a quiet corner to call Jared's wife.

"My son's a good doctor," Vinnie told Brynn, patting her hand in a grandfatherly manner that touched her. "Don't you be worrying about your friend."

The faintest lilt of an Italian accent in his gruff voice intrigued Brynn. All three of his sons sounded Texas born and raised, their surname and dark coloring the only hint of their heritage.

"Thank you, Mr. D'Alessandro. Everyone has been telling me that your son is a good surgeon. I believe it."

He nodded in satisfaction. "You call me 'Vinnie.' Everyone does."

She smiled. "Vinnie."

"My son said you're new to Dallas. From the number of boxes you had in your car, I assume you were moving here today."

Her smile faded. "We were going to spend tonight in a motel and start looking at apartments tomorrow."

It had seemed like such an adventure when she and Kelly left Longview earlier that day. They'd moved to Dallas to "seek their fortunes," as they'd told their friends. The future had seemed to spread in front of them like a sumptuous buffet waiting to be sampled.

They'd had no idea, of course, that everything would go so horribly wrong only minutes after they'd entered the Dallas city limits.

Vinnie frowned. "You don't even have a place to stay for tonight?"

Brynn ran a hand through her hair, wincing a bit

when her fingers brushed the tender lump at her temple. ''I'll worry about that after I find out how Kelly is.''

Vinnie opened his mouth to say something, but Brynn wouldn't have heard him had he spoken then.

Joe D'Alessandro had just entered the waiting room, his handsome face lined with exhaustion.

Brynn sprang to her feet, her heart leaping into her throat. She couldn't help noting the somberness in the doctor's dark eyes as he looked at her.

Oh, please. Let Kelly be all right, she prayed fervently. And then she stepped forward to meet Joe halfway.

Chapter Two

Joe had had little time to think of Brynn during the operation on her friend, but seeing her again affected him the same way it had before. Those crystal-blue eyes of hers were lethal, he mused, trying to hold on to his professional objectivity. When she looked at him, so worried and pleading, he found himself wanting to promise her anything, just to put a smile in those beautiful eyes.

He must be even more exhausted than he'd thought.

"Your friend is in Recovery," he said. "It will be a while yet before you can see her."

"Is she...?"

"She's resting," he said, when it was obvious that Brynn couldn't complete the question. "She has a concussion that causes us some concern, but we'll monitor her very closely for the next forty-eight hours or so. Her right arm was torn by a jagged piece of metal from her car door. It's been stitched and bandaged. She'll have a scar but should have full use of the arm back as soon as the cut heals. She has a clean break in her left femur, which I'll set as soon as the swelling goes down. Her most serious injury was to her right leg. I'm afraid that leg was basically crushed below the knee, to put it in layman's terms. She's got an uncomfortable recuperation ahead of her, with at least one more surgical procedure, and it's possible that she'll be left with a slight limp, but she *will* recover, Brynn. She's a very strong young woman.''

''Yes, she is,'' Brynn said with a faint sigh that might have expressed agreement, relief, weariness, distress or a combination of them all. ''When can I see her?''

''As soon as she's moved into a bed. You, er, said there's no one you want to call about the accident?''

''Not tonight. As I said, Kelly has no family. Her mother's dead and she hasn't seen or heard from her father since she was a little girl. She and I have considered ourselves sisters since we ended up in the same foster home when we were young girls. We like to say we're sisters by choice, rather than by blood.''

Few observers would have mistaken Brynn Larkin and Kelly Morrison for biological sisters, Joe thought. In contrast to Brynn's thick, dark brown mop of hair, fair, creamy skin and light-blue eyes, Kelly had fine, strawberry-blond hair, a gold-dusted complexion and emerald green eyes.

There were deep-purple hollows beneath Brynn's eyes now, he noted. Her face was pale, making her skin look even more like fine porcelain than he'd thought earlier. She needed rest, but he suspected she would refuse to leave the hospital until she'd seen Kelly.

''Where are you staying tonight?'' he asked, aware

that she had no transportation, and none of her things with her.

"With your mother and me," Vinnie said firmly, joining them in time to hear Joe's question. "You'll do us that honor, won't you, Brynn? My wife would love to meet you."

Joe watched Brynn's eyes widen, and he sensed that she was going to politely decline the invitation. He interceded quickly. "That's a good idea, Dad. Mom would strangle us if we let Brynn go off to a hotel by herself."

"Oh, but I—"

Winking at Joe, Vinnie nodded gravely. "My wife's a lovely woman, Ms. Larkin, but she'd take a broom to my sons and me if we didn't offer hospitality to someone in your situation. You can get some rest at our house tonight and tomorrow we'll see about finding you a place to stay."

"You'll like Carla D'Alessandro, Brynn," Jared seconded, joining them. "She's very nice, and her house is always open to guests. We'll all feel better knowing you have a comfortable place to stay for tonight."

Joe watched as Brynn looked around, finding herself surrounded by Vinnie, Jared, Shane, Tony and Michael, all smiling at her and urging her to accept Vinnie's invitation. He sensed the moment she surrendered to the benign pressure.

She made a little gesture of capitulation. "How can I refuse such a kind offer? If you're sure Mrs. D'Alessandro won't mind, I'll gratefully accept your hospitality."

Vinnie patted her shoulder, obviously quite pleased with her—and with himself. "I'll call Carla."

Brynn turned back to Joe. "I'd like to see Kelly before I go."

"Of course. I'll take you to her, though I can't promise she'll be entirely coherent."

"I just want to tell her good night."

He nodded.

Jared touched Brynn's arm. "You're in good hands now. I'd better head home."

Joe noticed a sudden brightness in Brynn's eyes when she looked up at Jared. "Thank you so much for everything you've done for me tonight."

Jared shrugged, looking typically uncomfortable with the expression of gratitude. "All I did was keep you company. And that was my pleasure."

Seeming to act on impulse, Brynn kissed Jared's cheek. "It meant a great deal to me."

To Joe's amusement, Jared blushed like a schoolboy.

Shane, never one to be left out of the spotlight for long, promptly stepped forward. "I brought you a cola," he reminded Brynn, presenting his cheek with an impudent grin that showcased his notorious dimples.

She smiled and brushed a quick kiss against his jaw. "Thank you."

Shane's expression turned smug. For some reason, Joe didn't find that little interplay nearly as amusing as the exchange between Brynn and Jared.

"I'll take you to Kelly," he said, taking a step closer to her side.

He was somewhat gratified to see that he immediately had her full attention.

He really was going to have to get some food and some rest. He wasn't behaving at all like himself, he thought with a sudden frown.

* * *

Brynn found herself suddenly almost reluctant to enter the room where Kelly lay. She was afraid of what she might see.

She looked nervously up at Joe, and saw he was watching her with a sympathetic expression. Funny. She'd always been a bit intimidated by doctors, had always found them difficult to talk to. Though something about him made her a little self-conscious at times, Joe didn't intimidate her. Instead, she was comforted by his presence, much as she had been by his friends and family earlier.

He reached around her and pushed open the door to Kelly's room. Brynn drew a deep breath and stepped inside.

Her first sight of Kelly forced the air from Brynn's lungs as effectively as a blow to the chest.

Kelly looked so young and vulnerable lying in the hospital bed, her bruised face still and pale, her arms at her sides, the left one pierced by an IV needle, the right swathed in bandages. Her legs were immobilized, the right one suspended in a daunting-looking contraption.

A hard sob ripped from Brynn's throat.

She wasn't aware that she had swayed until she felt Joe catch her shoulders. His hands were firm and warm through her sadly crumpled blouse. It was as if all the stress of the past hours finally caught up with her when she looked at Kelly lying in that bed. Brynn turned blindly and buried her face in Joe's shoulder, hardly aware of what she was doing. She *was* aware, however, that his arms immediately went around her, and that his warmth and his support were exactly the balm she needed at that moment.

"Kelly will be fine," he said, both compassion and understanding in his voice.

"She looks so...helpless."

"She looks much worse than she is at the moment. Concentrate on the good side, Brynn. When I first saw your car, I couldn't imagine that anyone sitting in the passenger seat would have survived. She's extremely fortunate that she's still alive. Considering the circumstances, you and Kelly were both lucky."

Brynn shuddered, thinking of how another few inches could have meant the difference in whether Kelly survived the crash or not. Joe's words had helped put everything back in perspective.

Joe.

Suddenly aware that she was standing in his arms, she wondered why she wasn't more embarrassed. She didn't even know this man, for goodness' sake. It wasn't like her to fall apart, to lean on strangers—particularly men. She could only attribute her behavior to the trauma of the accident.

She drew slowly out of his arms, wiping her face with the back of one hand and lifting her chin to show him she wasn't going to fall apart. "Thank you, Dr. D'Alessandro," she said, quietly and with whatever dignity she could summon, "for everything you've done for us."

His smile made her remember that he was an extremely attractive man, as well as a reputedly gifted surgeon—not that that made any difference, she assured herself hastily. "You're welcome."

A nurse carrying a medical chart entered the room. While Joe and the nurse conferred quietly about Kelly's care for the next few hours, Brynn stepped to the bed. Kelly was sleeping, the faintest crease between her brow indicating the pain she must be suffering, even subconsciously.

Brynn touched her friend's hand. It was so cold. So still, in heartbreaking contrast to Kelly's usual almost frenetic energy.

"Kelly?" Brynn didn't know if Kelly could hear her. "I just wanted you to know I'll be the leaving the hospital for a while. I'm going to spend the night with Dr. D'Alessandro's parents. They've all been very kind to me. I'll be back tomorrow, okay? They're going to take very good care of you here."

She brushed a lock of damp blond hair off Kelly's pale forehead. "If you need anything...*anything*...you ask for it, you hear? If you need me, they'll know how to reach me, okay?"

Joe stepped to Brynn's side but didn't touch her this time. "Are you ready?"

Brynn swallowed and nodded. "Good night, Kelly. Don't forget...T.W.R."

She drew a deep breath and turned to Joe. "I'm ready."

He studied her face a moment, then touched her arm, so fleetingly she hardly felt it. "Let's go."

Carla D'Alessandro was waiting to greet them when her husband and two sons ushered Brynn into the D'Alessandro home. A slender, olive-skinned woman with perfectly coiffed salt-and-pepper hair, she hardly looked old enough to have three grown sons, much less at least four grandchildren.

Brynn had been rather quiet during the ride from the hospital, letting Michael, Vinnie and Joe carry the conversation. As if sensing that she needed to be left to her thoughts for that brief interlude, the men hadn't tried to push her into contributing. Brynn had appreciated their thoughtfulness, just as she appreciated the welcome in Carla D'Alessandro's warm brown eyes.

Vinnie introduced Brynn to his wife.

"I'm so pleased you've agreed to be our guest tonight, Brynn," Carla said, her voice a rich, pleasing contralto. "I'm sorry about what happened to you and your friend. How are you feeling?"

"A little sore," Brynn admitted, responding instantly to the kindness in the older woman's face.

"And exhausted, no doubt. Michael, take Brynn to her things and let her point out the bags she'll need for tonight. Then carry them to the guest room for her. Joe, I know you're hungry, so go wash up while I get food on the table. You and Michael should eat before you head back to your place. Brynn, dear, I want you to make yourself at home. If you're hungry, the meal will be ready in a few minutes. Or feel free to take a hot bath and rest for a while, if you'd rather."

Amused at the evidence of who ruled the D'Alessandro household, Brynn replied, "Actually, I am rather hungry. Kelly and I..." She swallowed. "We were going to find a restaurant after we'd checked into a motel."

Her expression soft with compassion, Carla patted Brynn's arm. "Your friend will be all right, Brynn. My Joe is taking good care of her. Now, you let Michael show you to your things, and I'll get the food ready."

Twenty minutes later, they gathered around the table in Carla's beautifully decorated dining room. Carla had assembled a delicious cold meal of prosciutto, an assortment of cheeses, sliced fruit and crusty wheat bread that tasted homemade. Vinnie and Carla, who'd dined earlier, sipped cappuccinos and watched indulgently as the younger three devoured the food. Almost surprised that she still had an appetite after the events of the day, Brynn cleaned her plate but politely refused the cheesecake Carla offered for dessert.

Carla poured cappuccinos all around while Joe and Michael helped themselves to generous slices of cheesecake. "It's decaf," Carla said as she set a foamy mug in front of Brynn. "It shouldn't keep you awake."

Brynn smiled faintly. "I'm not sure anything could do that tonight."

She could feel the weariness pressing down on her, making her limbs feel heavy and her mind sluggish.

"I told my wife you and your friend are just moving to Dallas," Vinnie said, leaning back in his chair at the head of the table and studying Brynn with open curiosity.

She nodded. "Kelly's supposed to enter graduate school full-time at UT-Dallas in the fall, and I plan to take some evening classes toward my bachelor's degree. We moved here from Longview, where she received her undergraduate degree three weeks ago. I wasn't particularly happy in my job in Longview, and it wasn't hard for Kelly to talk me into moving here with her, so we could share an apartment while she earns her master's degree in communication disorders. She has a scholarship."

Suddenly deciding that she'd told them more than they'd probably wanted to know, she lifted her coffee mug to her mouth to shut herself up. Exhaustion and stress were making her babble.

But no one looked bored. They were all watching her as if waiting for her to expand further.

"What kind of work were you in?" Vinnie asked, apparently the official busybody in the family.

"I'm a licensed child-care worker. I love the work,

but I didn't care for the owner of the day-care center where I worked. I thought she was more focused on her profits than the children.''

''A child-care worker?'' Vinnie looked suddenly intrigued. ''Have you ever worked as a private nanny?''

Brynn noticed that the others seemed to follow Vinnie's question, as if they knew where he was leading. ''No, I haven't. My experience has been in day-care centers. I'm working toward a degree in elementary education, but I'm still a few years away from that, since I can only take evening classes while I support myself.''

''The reason I asked,'' Vinnie explained, ''is because my son and daughter—the ones who just had the new baby today—are looking for a nanny for their four children. Theirs just left them, at such an inconvenient time, with school just out and the new baby just arrived.''

''If you're interested, I'm sure Tony would like to talk to you about the job,'' Carla said to Brynn. ''But don't feel pressured, dear. There are many excellent day-care centers in Dallas, so you'll have no problem finding employment.''

Brynn had never actually considered being a nanny— she wasn't at all sure such a position could pay the salary she wanted, and many such positions were ''live-in,'' which didn't appeal to her. ''I'll give it some thought.''

''Not tonight,'' Joe said firmly. ''You've had enough to deal with today. Tonight, you need to rest and recuperate from the accident.''

He reached into the pocket of his shirt and pulled out a small white paper envelope, which he slid across the table to Brynn. ''I want you to take this pill before you go to bed.''

''What is it?''

Michael chuckled in response to Brynn's wary question. "Finally. Someone who doesn't just follow your orders blindly, *dottore*."

Ignoring his brother, Joe answered Brynn's question. "It's a mild muscle relaxer. It will help you sleep and relieve some of the soreness you're going to feel tomorrow."

Brynn nodded and slipped the pill into her pocket. She wouldn't promise to take it, but she would keep it close by in case she changed her mind.

She was so tired. It was all she could do to sit up straight in her seat, when all she wanted to do was to crawl into a warm bed and pretend the past six hours had never happened. If only she could wake to start the day over. She would drive more carefully next time, she vowed. She'd watch for vehicles going the wrong way. She'd sense that accidents were going to happen before they did. She...

Joe pushed his chair back from the table. "Let me walk you to the guest room."

Brynn didn't realize her eyelids had begun to droop until Joe's voice brought them wide-open again. "Oh. I..."

"You're falling asleep in your coffee," he said, his smile so kind it melted her resistance. "I'll walk you to your room, tell you a few things to watch for in the aftermath of your accident, then leave you to get some sleep. You can worry about all the other details tomorrow."

"Yes, Brynn, get some rest," Carla seconded warmly. "If there's anything you need during the night—anything at all—don't hesitate to ask, all right?"

Vinnie and Michael bade Brynn good-night, assuring her that they would be available to help her in any way they were needed. The kindness of this family toward a stranger in their midst was almost overwhelming to Brynn. She'd encountered true generosity all too rarely during her lifetime.

As if sensing that she was near collapse, Joe kept a hand beneath Brynn's elbow as he walked her to the guest room. It was a measure of her exhaustion that she found his touch so comfortable and almost familiar.

They paused together in front of the closed bedroom door.

"My mother was serious, you know. Anything you need, all you have to do is ask."

"Your family is very kind."

His smile was vaguely rueful. "Mom and Dad just love to get involved in other people's lives. Watch out for Dad especially. There's nothing he likes better than taking a new chick under his wing. He'll be giving you advice and suggestions until you ask him to butt out."

"I'll gladly listen to his advice," Brynn responded with a weak smile in return. "I'm taking all the suggestions I can get right now."

"Yeah, well, you've never encountered anyone like my pop. Ever since he took early retirement from his career as a private investigator—and that was more than ten years ago—his favorite hobby has been running the lives of his family members. And he defines family very loosely. You're spending a night in his house. That makes you family, in his opinion."

Brynn was appalled to feel her eyes suddenly fill with tears. She had never belonged to a large, supportive family like this one. Even Joe's mild teasing about his was enough to renew an old, empty ache in her heart. She averted her face quickly, before he could see.

"You said you wanted to talk to me about the accident?"

"Yeah. You've done very well this evening, considering everything, but you're going to be sore as he...er, heck, tomorrow. You took a hard jolt when that truck hit your car. Your seat belt slammed you back against your seat—exactly as it's designed to do—your head hit the window, your neck and spine were jarred. You're going to feel like someone beat you with a stick."

Her precarious emotions under control, Brynn glanced at him with a wry smile. "Don't sugarcoat it, Doctor. Give it to me straight."

He smiled at her quip but continued to speak seriously. "Take the pill I gave you. It will help you relax, help you sleep. A hot bath wouldn't be a bad idea, either, but don't stay in it too long. It'll sap whatever strength you have left."

She nodded and turned the doorknob, opening the door an inch or so. "Thank you, Doctor."

"'Joe,'" he said, the reminder sounding just a bit irritable. "I'm not on the time clock. Just making suggestions."

She couldn't help smiling again. "You must have gotten that trait from your father."

He winced, then chuckled. "Yeah, I probably did. Anyway, if you have any problems other than the ones I've described...sudden headache or dizziness... anything at all...you let my parents know, all right? I live about twenty minutes away, but I can be here in less if you need me."

"I'll be fine. Thank you, Joe. I don't know how I'll repay you for all you've done."

He touched her arm and smiled. "I told you, I'm not

on the time clock now. The insurance companies will take care of everything else.''

She wasn't sure whether her sudden light-headedness was a result of her exhaustion, his touch or his smile. Maybe a combination. Whatever the cause, it was time for her to put some space between herself and this attractive doctor, at least until she had cleared her head and pulled all her natural defenses back into place. She was confident that a good night's sleep would help her with both.

''Good night,'' she said, pushing the door open and stepping quickly away from his hand. ''Thank you again.''

She had the door closed behind her before he could reply.

Surprisingly enough, Brynn didn't lie awake, tossing and turning and fretting about Kelly's injuries or worrying about their future or trying to get used to her strange surroundings. She was unconscious almost as soon as her head hit the pillow, and her sleep was deep, dreamless. The only time she roused during the night was when a soft hand touched her forehead.

Blinking her eyes against the dim glow of a nightlight, Brynn peered up into the smiling face of Carla D'Alessandro.

''I hope I didn't frighten you,'' Carla said softly. ''I just wanted to make sure you're all right. Despite Joe's reassurances, that bruise on your head made me worry about a concussion.''

''I'm fine,'' Brynn croaked, her voice still hoarse from sleep. ''But thank you for being concerned.''

''I raised three accident-prone sons,'' Carla explained. ''I became so accustomed to getting up in the night and holding up fingers for them to count that the habit just seemed to stick with me.''

Brynn thought of all the nights she'd lain in bed as a child, wishing she had the kind of mother who would tuck her in and check on her. ''Your sons are very fortunate,'' she murmured.

''I've always thought it was the other way around. Good night, Brynn.''

''G'night, Mrs. D'Alessandro.''

'''Carla.''' With that gentle reminder, the older woman slipped out of the room. Brynn went back to sleep with a wistful smile playing on her lips.

''She's pretty.''

Joe twisted the key in the lock of his front door and tried to concentrate on his brother's words. Michael was visiting from Austin in honor of his new nephew's arrival and had already planned to bunk at Joe's place for the night. They'd been on their way here when they'd seen the wreck that had so radically changed their plans for the evening.

''What did you say, Mike?''

''Brynn Larkin. I said she's very attractive.''

Joe pushed open the door. ''Oh? Yes, I suppose so.''

''As if you didn't notice.'' Michael openly scoffed at Joe's attempt at nonchalance. ''You nearly swallowed your tongue every time she smiled.''

''Give me a break. She's at least ten years younger than I am. And she's my patient.''

''Brynn's not your patient. Her friend is. I saw the way you watched Brynn during dinner.''

All his life, Joe had been the butt of teasing from his elder brothers. All his life, he'd been trying to learn not to let their teasing get to him. He still hadn't quite learned the trick.

"I wasn't looking at her in any particular way, other than to make sure she was okay. I'm really not in the mood for this, Mike."

"Okay, fine. I just couldn't help noticing, that's all."

"And I can't help noticing that you're nuts. I'm going to bed. You know where everything is, right? Don't need me to tuck you into the guest bed?"

Michael answered with a mild Italian obscenity. But his attention didn't stray long from his original subject. "Did you notice her eyes?"

"Michael…"

"No, seriously. They were such a light blue. Crystal, almost. They reminded me of someone. Can't think who just now."

"You think about that. I've got to get some sleep."

Joe crawled into bed half an hour later, so tired his hair ached. But as he pulled the sheets around him, he found himself thinking of Brynn Larkin. She really *was* pretty. And her eyes were familiar.

Who…?

He fell asleep before he could decide exactly who Brynn's light-blue eyes reminded him of.

Chapter Three

Even before Brynn looked at the clock Sunday morning, she knew she'd slept later than she had intended. She gasped when she saw the time. Ten o'clock! She hadn't slept this late in years. Just what had been in that pill Joe had given her last night?

She tossed off the covers and shoved herself upright, then gasped again when every abused muscle in her body protested the abrupt movement. Joe had said the pill would ease the soreness she would feel this morning. How much worse could it have been if she *hadn't* taken it?

Moving very carefully, she stood and shuffled into the bathroom. She couldn't help thinking of Precious, her foster mother's old, arthritic pug. The dog had lived to be nearly eighteen and had always reminded Brynn and Kelly of a crotchety old lady. Now Brynn understood a bit better why poor old Precious had been such a grouch.

A hot shower helped a bit. Conscious of passing time, Brynn didn't linger long under the soothing spray. She grimaced when she caught a glimpse of her reflection as she stepped carefully out of the shower. Her skin was blotched with purple bruises, and her complexion looked sallow even through the mirror fog. It was just as well, she thought with a rueful smile, that no one else was around to see her just then. Not that there was anyone in particular she wanted to see her naked, even at her best, she thought with a blush, pushing a mental image of an attractive, dark-eyed doctor out of her mind. Where had that thought come from, anyway?

She dressed as quickly as she could in a long-sleeved, navy-and-white knit pullover and pleated navy slacks, an outfit she selected for comfort and because it had survived a night in a suitcase without accumulating too many wrinkles. She blew her hair into her usual smooth bob, tried to add some color to her face with makeup, then decided she was as ready as she was going to be to face her hosts.

She found Vinnie settled into a big leather chair in the den, the Sunday paper spread around him. He looked up over his reading glasses with a smile. "*Buon giorno,* Brynn. How are you feeling?"

"Fine, thank you," she fibbed with a smile in return. "I can't believe I slept so late."

"Joe said you needed your rest."

Joe said. Apparently, that was all the explanation required. It couldn't have been more obvious that the D'Alessandros had a great deal of pride and confidence in the doctor in their family.

"Brynn, good morning." Carla entered the room

wiping her hands on a dish towel. "Did you sleep well?"

"Very well, thank you."

"I just talked to Joe. He's on his way over to join us for brunch."

"Has he checked on Kelly this morning?"

Carla nodded. "As a matter of fact, he called from the hospital. He said he'd spent some time with her this morning and she's doing very well, considering what she went through yesterday. He can give you more specific information when he gets here, which should be any minute now."

Brynn felt a kick of nerves in her stomach at the thought of Joe's imminent arrival. She told herself she was only anxious to hear about Kelly. "Is Michael coming for brunch, as well?"

Carla shook her head. "Michael had to leave early this morning to go back to Austin, to his wife and little girl. He has a big case coming up tomorrow, and he needed a bit more time to prepare. He only made a short visit to welcome the new baby. He stopped by here on his way to the airport to tell you goodbye, but you were still sleeping and we didn't want to disturb you."

"I'm sorry I missed him. He was very kind to me yesterday."

"We've raised all our boys to help those in need," Vinnie announced with gruff pride. "They take after their parents."

Carla rolled her eyes. "Forgive my husband's immodesty," she murmured. "Humility has never been one of his virtues."

Vinnie waved a hand to dismiss his wife's mild criticism. "Like their parents," he continued firmly, "they've all chosen professions that offer service to others. Joe's a doctor, of course. Michael followed his mother into the legal profession—did we mention that Carla's a judge?''

"No, you didn't." Impressed—and now a bit intimidated—Brynn glanced at Carla.

Carla smiled. "I'm thinking of retiring next year, when I turn seventy."

Seventy? Brynn had underestimated Carla's age by a minimum of five years.

"And Tony's a private investigator," Vinnie continued, his chest puffing out a tiny bit more.

"Joe told me that you are a former private investigator."

Vinnie nodded. "Retired. Tony followed his old man's example…first into the police academy, then into his own business. He's got a big investigation and security agency here in Dallas. Very successful. Highly respected."

"And my husband will brag about his sons all day, if we let him," Carla cut in. "Which we won't."

Brynn only smiled, thinking it was nice that Vinnie was so proud of his family. She couldn't help acknowledging that this was exactly the type of family she'd fantasized about belonging to as a child. She wondered if Tony, Michael and Joe truly understood how lucky they were.

As if in response to her thoughts, Joe strolled through the door at that moment. Brynn caught her breath at the sight of him. She'd almost forgotten how very attractive this man was, with his thick dark hair that showed an endearing tendency to curl at the ends, his gleaming dark eyes, his sexy smile and loose-limbed walk that was almost a swagger.

She told herself that it was okay to appreciate his

masculine assets as long as she didn't start weaving any fantasies about the smiles he gave her—the same smiles he gave *all* women, she suspected.

It was a good thing that she'd reminded herself not to take him too seriously. Had she not, she might have been a bit flattered by the way he walked immediately to stand close in front of her, searching her face with warm, intense eyes, and with apparently sincere concern in his voice when he asked, "How are you? Did you rest well?"

"Yes, I'm fine. How's Kelly?"

"She's doing very well," he assured her. "She's in some pain, but that's to be expected. I promised her I'd take you to her as soon as you've had a chance to eat. Oh, and she sent you a message. 'T.W.R.'?"

Brynn smiled at his slightly puzzled expression. "Thank you. I understand."

Joe nodded. "Then I must have delivered it correctly."

"Did you see the baby this morning?" Carla asked Joe.

He glanced away from Brynn long enough to smile at his mother. "He's doing great. As is his mother. Michelle was nagging to go home when I saw her right after they served her breakfast."

Carla clucked in disapproval. "She's only been in the hospital twenty-four hours. She shouldn't be in such a rush, especially since this one had to be a difficult C-section delivery. It wouldn't hurt her to take another night to rest and recuperate."

"I, er, mentioned something like that to her. She said she's thirty-seven years old and the mother of four children, and that she's perfectly capable of taking care of herself at home. I'm not so sure her doctor agrees, though. He wants to keep her another night, if he can convince her to cooperate.''

With a sigh, Carla shook her head. ''That Michelle. So stubborn.''

Joe chuckled. ''She fits right into this family.''

Brynn crossed her arms and tucked her hands into her elbows, a habit she'd developed in childhood when she felt awkward or left out—a condition that usually hit her whenever others talked about their families. Whether because she was unusually perceptive or just trying to be a gracious hostess, Carla brought the conversation to an end then, ushering Brynn and the others into the dining room for the delectable brunch she had prepared.

Brynn was rather surprised at the comfortable, yet simple, life-style the elder D'Alessandros seemed to live. She would have thought a judge would live in more luxurious circumstances.

Not that she'd ever met a judge. But Carla D'Alessandro just didn't fit Brynn's mental image of the word.

With an effort, she reined in her impatience to see her injured friend—as well as her vague sense of guilt that she was about to have a lovely brunch with a very nice family while Kelly was lying in a hospital room.

Vinnie seemed to sense where Brynn's thoughts centered during the meal. ''How long have you and Kelly known each other, Brynn?''

''Almost twelve years. Since I was fourteen and she was almost eleven. I'd been living in a foster home since my mother…died a year earlier, and Kelly moved in when her mother became too ill to take care of her. Kelly's mother died a couple of years later. Neither of us had any other relatives, but we were fortunate to be able to remain in the same foster home until we both graduated from high school. From the beginning, Kelly was like my little sister. We've been together ever since.''

Again, she'd found herself answering with more detail than had been absolutely necessary, but this family was so easy to talk to. They seemed so interested in what she had to say.

''Was it a good foster home?'' Vinnie wanted to know.

Brynn nodded matter-of-factly. ''Mrs. Fendel was strict but well-intentioned. And after Kelly arrived, it wasn't so lonely.''

Joe reached for his coffee cup, calling Brynn's attention to him. She found him watching her over the rim, the expression in his eyes hard to read.

She cleared her throat and looked quickly away.

''We know several people who were raised in the foster home environment,'' Carla commented, apparently unaware of the sudden tension between Brynn and Joe—or was Brynn the only one who felt it? ''For some, it was a positive experience, for others it wasn't.''

Brynn shrugged lightly, trying without success to ignore the all-too-intriguing man across the table from her. ''For me, it was positive, I suppose. I had a safe, comfortable home to grow up in, and I met Kelly. I went into the foster home having no family at all, and I left with a sister.''

''You were the first one she asked about when I saw her this morning,'' Joe said. ''She didn't ask about her own injuries until she'd made sure that you were all right.''

Brynn had to look down at her plate for a moment before she was certain her voice was steady when she answered. "As I said, it's been just the two of us for a long time. When you only have one person to call family, you worry about…about losing that person, and being left with…"

No one.

Brynn couldn't say the words. She was still so sharply aware of how closely she had come to losing her dearest friend that she couldn't even talk about it yet.

Carla's hand covered Brynn's on the table. "Kelly will be fine, Brynn. You haven't lost her."

Brynn tried to smile. She looked at Joe, making no effort to hide her gratitude. "I know. Thanks to your sons."

She was rather surprised when Joe suddenly frowned and changed the subject. "Have you heard from Tia Luisa since the new baby arrived?"

Vinnie chuckled. "She called yesterday. My aunt," he added for Brynn's benefit. "Ninety-four years old and she can run circles around any of us. She's the terror of the family. She wanted to know when we're bringing the baby to see her. I told her he isn't even out of the hospital yet, but she said that was no excuse."

"And I suppose she's annoyed that Tony and Michelle didn't name the baby Leonardo?" Joe asked with a wry grin.

Again, Vinnie made sure Brynn was included in the joke. "Tia Luisa's father…my grandfather…was named Leonardo. I'm the eldest grandson, and she thinks one of my grandchildren should be named after their great-grandfather. Actually, she's still annoyed because I didn't name any of my sons Leonardo. And, since Michael has only the one daughter and Joe hasn't yet done his duty to marry and produce more

D'Alessandro heirs, it was up to Tony to give in to her demands.''

Joe's grin deepened. ''Tony's too stubborn to give in. He says he'll darned well name his kids whatever he likes. And he doesn't like the name Leonardo. If he wasn't Tia Luisa's favorite, she probably wouldn't be speaking to him now.''

''Luisa isn't partial to Tony,'' Carla murmured.

Joe snorted his disbelief. ''She's batty about him. And he's the same way about her. Which is why he takes such warped pleasure in ticking her off.''

''Actually, I rather like the name Leonardo,'' Brynn mused, thinking of a certain gorgeous actor she and Kelly both admired.

Joe grimaced. ''A lot of young women seem to like that name these days.''

Brynn laughed. ''What can I say? We're suckers for a sexy smile.''

Joe was looking at her mouth as he set his empty coffee cup down. Rather than responding to her quip, he changed the subject yet again. ''Whenever you're finished with your meal, I'll take you to see your friend.''

Brynn turned her attention quickly back to her meal, wanting to finish every bite so she wouldn't hurt Carla's feelings.

Brynn and Joe talked mostly about Kelly's medical condition during the drive to the hospital. Brynn noticed that Joe was in ''doctor mode'' during the entire drive, as if he'd left his personal life behind at his parents' house and became the ultimate professional on the way to his work venue. She even found herself calling him ''Doctor'' again, rather than ''Joe.''

She noticed he didn't correct her. She told herself it was just as well. She'd been imagining undercurrents between her and Joe that were highly improbable, now that she stopped to think about it. Even if she were looking for a relationship, which she most definitely was *not,* she couldn't imagine a more unlikely pairing than her and Dr. Joe D'Alessandro.

"When will Kelly be able to leave the hospital?" she asked as Joe drove into the parking lot.

"It will be a minimum of four weeks," he answered, his tone gentle. "Possibly six."

Brynn digested his answer in stunned silence. Four to six weeks. The bills were going to be astronomical. Joe and the others had reassured her that the other driver's insurance would cover the expenses, since there was no doubt that the intoxicated man had been at fault, having a history of driving under the influence behind him, but still...

Brynn and Kelly had intended to stay in a motel for a few days until they found a relatively inexpensive, furnished apartment. Now Brynn was on her own for at least a month, probably more. What would she do?

Brynn almost ran to Kelly's hospital room, Joe following a bit more sedately behind her. Prepared now for what she would see inside, she pushed open the door.

Kelly was awake this time. Her face was almost as white as the pillowcase when she turned her head to see who had entered the room

"If it isn't the hospital heartthrob," she murmured, looking at Joe.

The teasing comment reassured Brynn somewhat. It was so very characteristic of her friend.

To Brynn's amusement, Joe's cheeks darkened. "I

can tell you're going to be a problem patient," he muttered.

She smiled. "Bet on it."

Kelly looked at Brynn then and held out her left hand, the one with the IV needle taped above it. "Brynn. Your face is bruised. Are you all right?"

That was almost Brynn's undoing. Poor Kelly was lying battered and broken in the hospital bed, and she was worried about the bruise on her friend's temple. Blinking rapidly against a threatening wave of tears, Brynn forced a smile, and caught Kelly's hand in her own. "I'm fine. How are *you?*"

"Not so bad," Kelly lied shamelessly, her voice slurred by medication. "Everyone's been really nice to me here. I've already had visitors this morning, and made some new friends."

"Oh? Who visited you?"

"Dr. Joe, of course." Kelly smiled again at Joe. "And his brother Tony stepped in early this morning when he came to see his wife and the new baby. And later, Jared Walker and his wife, Cassie, came by to introduce themselves and tell me to let them know if we needed anything. Jared said he met you yesterday."

"Jared sat with me during your surgery. He's a nice man."

"They're a very nice couple. So sweet and concerned. What did you do, Brynn, tell everyone I'm a poor, wounded orphan?"

Knowing Kelly was teasing, Brynn tried to smile. "Well, aren't you?"

"Yeah, but did you have to hang a sign?"

"Seemed like the most efficient way to get the word out."

Kelly shifted her weight on the bed, and her smile faded into a grimace. "Ouch."

Brynn tightened her hand around Kelly's. "Are you okay? Joe?"

Even as Joe stepped quickly forward, Kelly made a face and carefully shook her head against the pillow. "It's no big deal, Brynn. I've got a stitched-up arm and two broken legs and a few other assorted bumps and bruises. It's only natural that there's going to be some discomfort, so don't worry so much."

"She's right, Brynn," Joe said reassuringly, though he was looking at Kelly closely. "Kelly's going to have some pain, but she's doing quite well."

"I'm fine," Kelly repeated firmly. "Just…a little tired," she admitted.

"You need plenty of rest," Joe said. "I'm going to go check on a couple other patients. You and Brynn can visit for a little while, and then you can get some sleep, Kelly."

Kelly nodded. "Thanks, Dr. Joe."

He glanced back over his shoulder as he left the room. "See you later."

The words were directed to both of them, but he was looking at Brynn when he spoke.

"He's great, isn't he?" Kelly said as soon as the door had closed behind Joe.

Realizing she'd been staring at that closed door, Brynn turned quickly back to the bed. "Dr. D'Alessandro? Yes, he's very nice."

"I can't get over how kind everyone has been," Kelly murmured, her eyes half-closed. "I think we're going to like Dallas."

"I think you're right." Brynn spoke gently, keeping her voice low. "Though I don't expect everyone here to be as nice as the D'Alessandro and Walker families. We were just lucky to meet them yesterday.''

"I'd hate to think of you sitting alone in that waiting room yesterday, then trying to find a motel to stay in by yourself.''

"So would I.''

"What happened to our things?''

"Mr. and Mrs. D'Alessandro—Dr. D'Alessandro's parents—are storing everything in their garage for now. Vinnie—Mr. D'Alessandro—has promised to help me get a rental car tomorrow and find a place to stay. I'm afraid you're going to be here for a while yet, but I hope to at least have an apartment by the time you get out.''

"Mr. D'Alessandro sounds very helpful.''

"Yes. He's retired, and Joe—er, Dr. D'Alessandro—implied that his father is always looking for things to do to keep him busy. You and I seem to be his new project.''

"We're lucky,'' Kelly repeated, her eyelids growing heavier.

Brynn looked at the bandages and bruises, the IV needle and splints, and knew she should find it strange that Kelly kept repeating how lucky they were. But, remembering the accident and knowing how it could have ended, Brynn tended to agree. She and Kelly *had* been lucky.

They still had each other. And now they seemed to have some new friends. All in all, it could have been much, much worse.

Kelly fell asleep less than ten minutes later. Brynn sat beside her, watching her sleep and worrying about the future, until Joe returned shortly afterward.

"She's sleeping," Brynn said unnecessarily, nodding toward her friend.

"Best thing for her right now. The pain medications she's on will keep her very groggy for a few days. I've also got her on a strong antibiotic. We want to avoid any infection setting up in her wounds."

Brynn twisted her hands in her lap, keeping her eyes on Kelly's still form. "I don't know what to do."

"For Kelly, you mean? She's being well cared for, Brynn."

Brynn shook her head. "I know she has good care here. But..."

"You're worried about what you should do next?" he supplied perceptively.

Brynn nodded. "I don't have a car or a place to live or a job. I don't know what to do next... I don't even know what I should be doing right now."

"Resting," Joe answered firmly. "You were in the same serious accident Kelly was in yesterday. You can't expect to rebound from that overnight, even if your injuries were minor. As for the rest, don't worry about it today. There isn't a whole lot you can do on a Sunday afternoon, anyway. And as for having a place to live, you're welcome to stay with my parents until you find something more permanent. They're expecting you to do so."

"I can't keep imposing on your family," Brynn protested. "I'm sure they have things to do other than entertain an uninvited guest."

"You are not an uninvited guest. I was standing right beside you when Dad invited you, remember? I told you, my folks love having someone to fuss over. They like you, I can tell."

Brynn managed a smile, telling herself she should

stop complaining and show her gratitude for the help she'd been given. "I like them, too."

"Then stop worrying, okay?"

She wasn't making promises she knew she couldn't keep. "I'll try."

Joe glanced at Kelly again. She was still sleeping soundly. "How would you like to meet my new nephew?" he asked Brynn. "He's a great-looking kid. Takes after his uncle, I think," he added, obviously trying to make her smile.

"I would love to see your new nephew," she agreed, because she could tell he genuinely wanted to show the baby off.

She loved looking through nursery windows at newborns. They were so tiny and sweet when they were only hours old. They made such amusing faces. She couldn't imagine a better distraction from her worries about her uncertain future.

Joe opened the door. "Let's go, then."

With one last glance at Kelly, Brynn preceded Joe out of the room.

Brynn hesitated outside the door to Michelle's hospital room, looking disconcerted.

Joe glanced at her in question. "What's wrong?"

"I, er, thought you were taking me to the nursery to see your nephew through the glass."

"No, Michelle has him in her room with her."

"Maybe I should…"

He reached out and caught her hand, squeezing reassuringly. He found Brynn's occasional flashes of shyness rather endearing. "You've already met Tony. And Michelle has said she would like to meet you. Let me introduce you."

Brynn drew a deep breath and nodded. "All right."

Tony stood from the chair beside his wife's bed as soon as Joe led Brynn in. He stepped forward with a smile of welcome. "Ms. Larkin—Brynn. It's good to see you again. How is Kelly?"

"She's resting now."

"I'd like you to meet my family. Michelle, this is Brynn Larkin."

Her usual grace and charm in evidence even from her hospital bed, Michelle spoke warmly. "Tony told me all about you. I'm so sorry about your accident. Are you all right?"

"Yes, I'm fine, thank you. Just a little stiff."

Tony motioned toward one of the two chairs in the room. "Please, have a seat. You, too, Joe. I'll sit here, on the edge of the bed."

He waited until Joe and Brynn had taken their seats before introducing his curious children to Brynn. "This is our eldest, Jason," he said, nodding toward the nine-year-old boy who'd already moved close to Joe's side. "And our daughters, Carly and Katie. And the runt of the litter, here, is Justin."

It was obvious from the way she smiled at them that Brynn had a fondness for children. "Hello. You must all be very proud of your new baby brother."

Jason spoke up first. "I'm going to teach him to play baseball. Of course, it's going to be a while."

Brynn nodded gravely. "Sooner than you think. What position do you play?"

"First base. But I want to pitch. I've been practicing real hard."

"Anything worth doing requires a lot of hard work."

Jason glanced at Tony. "That's what my daddy says."

Six-year-old Carly sidled closer to Brynn. "I got a loose tooth," she said, enthusiastically wiggling it with the tip of one finger. Joe knew Carly was eager to reclaim the attention her new little brother had temporarily grabbed.

Brynn focused obligingly on Carly. "My goodness, it is loose, isn't it? I have a feeling you'll be getting a visit from the tooth fairy soon."

"He brought Jason a whole dollar for his last tooth."

"Wow. Maybe I should pull a couple of mine."

Carly giggled. "The tooth fairy doesn't come see big people. Only kids."

Brynn sighed deeply. "Then I suppose I'd better keep my teeth."

The shyest of the D'Alessandro clan, four-year-old Katie inched tentatively closer to Brynn's chair. She aimed a plastic rectangle at Brynn's face, directing a narrow beam of light straight into Brynn's eyes. "I got a flashlight."

Brynn shifted subtly in her chair. "That's a nice, bright light."

"Not in her eyes, Katie," Tony murmured.

Katie pointed the beam at the floor. "Uncle Joe gave it to me," she informed Brynn.

Brynn smiled at Joe. "That was very nice of him."

Katie frowned and shook her head. "Not *Dr.* Joe. *Uncle* Joe."

Tony chuckled in response to Brynn's obvious incomprehension. "Michelle and I both have brothers named Joe," he explained. "To distinguish them, the kids call mine 'Dr. Joe' and Michelle's brother 'Uncle Joe.'"

"We've gotten used to it," *Dr.* Joe added with a shrug of resignation.

Brynn looked at Michelle. "I met your brother Jared yesterday. He was kind enough to sit with me during my friend's surgery."

Michelle's face softened. "Jared has a way of making you believe everything's going to be all right, doesn't he?"

"Yes," Brynn admitted. "He does."

"Shane lets me ride his horse," Carly piped up.

Brynn turned back to the children. "Does he?"

"Me, too," Katie said, not to be outdone.

Joe watched as the children surrounded Brynn, all talking at once, pushing closer and closer to her chair, obviously responding to her smile and her genuine interest in what they had to say. So he wasn't the only one who felt drawn toward her. Interesting.

He glanced at Tony and Michelle, noting that they were watching with interest as their children bonded with Brynn. He suspected it wouldn't be long before Tony and Michelle offered Brynn the position their nanny had recently vacated. And considering Brynn's need for immediate employment, she would probably accept…which meant that Joe would be seeing her whenever he visited his brother and sister-in-law.

He knew he was headed for trouble when he found himself thinking that he really hadn't spent enough time at Tony and Michelle's house lately.

Chapter Four

Brynn was amused when Katie suddenly turned to her uncle with big, adoring eyes. "Ice cream, Dr. Joe?"

Joe's mouth quirked. "Is this a sudden craving you've developed?"

Obviously having little idea what he meant, Katie nodded anyway. "Ice cream."

"Katie," Michelle murmured repressively.

Joe chuckled and shook his head. "I'll take these three for a quick ice cream down in the canteen. Brynn, you want ice cream or would you rather stay and visit a while with Michelle and Tony?"

"Oh, I…"

"Please stay, Brynn," Michelle said quickly. "Tony and I would love to get to know you better."

Remembering that Vinnie had said Tony and Michelle were looking for a new nanny, and wondering if he'd already mentioned to them that Brynn had experience in that line of work, she nodded a bit hesitantly. "All right."

Joe held out his hands to the girls, then motioned for Jason to follow. "We won't be long," he promised.

"Doesn't Justin want ice cream?" Katie asked innocently.

Jason rolled his eyes, the exasperated older brother. "Babies can't eat ice cream, Katie."

Katie sighed and looked sympathetically at the infant in her mother's arms. "Poor baby."

Brynn felt a need to say something as the door closed behind Joe and the children. "They're obviously quite fond of their uncle. And it's obviously mutual."

Michelle nodded. "Yes. Joe loves all the children. The girls, especially, have him wrapped around their fingers. All Carly or Katie have to do is smile at him and bat their lashes, and he's putty in their hands."

Brynn clasped her fingers in front of her, thinking with a slight pang that Joe would probably make a wonderful father. She wondered why he'd not yet married and started a family. Had he been too busy establishing his medical career? Or had he simply not met anyone he wanted to be the mother of his children?

She imagined there were any number of eligible women who wouldn't mind discussing the possibility with him.

She pushed thoughts of Joe's romantic life out of her mind, since it had absolutely nothing to do with her. "You mentioned you have a brother named Joe, Michelle," she said, still trying to make conversation. "Do you have other brothers or sisters besides Jared?"

"There are six of us. Jared, Layla, Joe, Ryan and Lindsay."

"Six." Brynn shook her head. "It must have been

wonderful growing up with so many brothers and sisters to play with," she murmured, a bit wistfully.

Michelle suddenly wore an odd expression. "I... um..." She moistened her lips. "That's a rather long story. Actually, Tony and I wanted to talk to you about something else."

She glanced from her baby to her husband and then back at Brynn. "We understand that you're a child-care worker. Vinnie mentioned that we're looking for a nanny?"

"Yes, he did."

"Maybe we'd better tell you exactly what we need," Tony said. "Michelle works as charity administrator for Trent Enterprises, a corporation based here in Dallas. She works out of our home primarily, but her work keeps her very busy. She needs someone to help her entertain the kids during the days while she works. It isn't a live-in position—we take care of the children in the evenings and at night. But we're willing to pay very well for someone we can trust with our children, someone who's qualified to entertain and stimulate them while they're home from school."

He named a figure that made Brynn blink. It was as much as she'd made working full-time for the day-care center in Longview. "I—uh..."

Michelle made a face. "We're rather desperate, actually. My sister Layla is helping with the children this weekend, but she has to work tomorrow, and Tony can only take another day or two away from his office. I'm not supposed to do much lifting for the next few weeks, and I'll need some help."

Tony spoke again. "We know you'll need a place to stay. Michelle and I are prepared to offer you our guest house for as long as you need it. It's small but furnished. Michelle's family's housekeeper and gardener used to live there, but it's been unoccupied since they retired several years ago.''

Brynn stared at the earnest-looking couple gazing back at her. ''You don't even know me,'' she couldn't help protesting. ''What makes you think I'm qualified to take care of your children?''

Michelle smiled. ''We consider ourselves pretty fair judges of character. So do Vinnie and Carla. They like you. And I've just seen for myself that you're wonderful with children.''

Brynn frowned, suddenly remembering exactly what Tony D'Alessandro did for a living. ''Have you investigated me?''

Tony's lips quirked. ''I haven't had time to investigate you. Would I find anything to disturb me if I did?''

''No,'' Brynn answered candidly. ''Actually, you'd find out that I have a spotless reputation. Quitting my job at the day-care center in Longview and moving here with Kelly is the most impulsive and adventurous thing I've ever done.''

Michelle's smile deepened. ''Then there's no problem, is there?''

''We know things are very unsettled for you right now,'' Tony said. ''We certainly don't expect you to make a decision like this on the spot. I'll be around to help Michelle for a few days. Maybe you'd like to think about it for a while before giving an answer.''

Brynn was tempted to accept immediately. She needed the job, the salary and the place to live. She already liked the D'Alessandro children. It all sounded ideal. But she knew Tony was right about her needing time to think before she agreed. Everything had happened so quickly since the accident.

Little Justin seemed to grow tired of being ignored He squirmed and mewed, one tiny hand escaping his blanket to flail irritably in the air. Unable to resist, Brynn stood and walked closer to the bed for a better look at the baby.

"He's so beautiful," she breathed, staring at perfect pink skin, tight black curls and glittering dark eyes.

Michelle and Tony preened in unison.

"Would you like to hold him?" Michelle asked.

Brynn ached to hold him. "I..."

Before she could politely demur, Michelle had already deposited her son in Brynn's arms.

Justin blinked up at Brynn as if trying to decide whether this was a new face or one he'd seen before. His mouth pursed, then opened for another experimental squeak.

The feeling of holding this tiny, perfect, brand-new person was staggering. It was as if she were holding pure joy. But the joy was mixed with a touch of old anguish that she would never hold a child of her own.

The door opened and Justin's siblings burst in, beaming faces bearing evidence of chocolate ice cream. Joe followed a bit more sedately.

Brynn quickly but carefully transferred the baby back to his mother.

"I'd better go check on Kelly again," she said, suddenly needing to be away from this kind, but somewhat overwhelming, family.

Joe nodded. "I'll take you to her."

"We'll talk again in the next day or two," Tony said to Brynn, and she knew he was referring to their offer of a job. They would need an answer soon.

She only wished she knew what that answer should be.

* * *

"Can I get you anything else to eat, Brynn? Another piece of pie?"

Brynn couldn't help laughing a little, even as she pressed a hand to her stomach. "Thank you, Carla, but I couldn't eat another bite."

"Cappuccino?"

"No, thank you."

Vinnie looked over the newsmagazine he'd been reading in his easy chair. "Stop pestering the girl, Carla. She's fine."

Carla sent her husband a look and reopened the book she'd been reading. "I was just asking."

"And I appreciate it," Brynn assured her, smiling.

She glanced down at the notepad in her lap, studying the list she'd been working on. She was trying to make a note of everything she needed to do the next day, from contacting the insurance company again to renting a car to picking up some things for Kelly. Brynn had always been a list maker, a trait Kelly often teased her about.

"Joe said you met Tony and Michelle today," Vinnie murmured from behind the magazine, his tone studiously casual.

"Yes. The children, as well."

"Did you like them?"

"They seem like a very nice family."

"I, er, mentioned to them that you might be available for the nanny job."

"Now who's pestering the girl?" Carla asked pointedly.

Vinnie closed the magazine. "I'm only making conversation."

"You're prying."

"I am not prying. If I were prying, I would ask her

if Tony had offered her the job. And then I would ask if she accepted.''

"Face it, you're prying. And I wouldn't blame Brynn a bit if she told you to mind your own business.''

Brynn cleared her throat. "Um—''

Vinnie blustered. "She's much too polite to do such a thing. Just as I would not be so rude as to ask about her personal business. Although, if she *wanted* to talk about it, I certainly wouldn't stop her.''

"Well, I—''

Carla spoke over Brynn's attempt to intercede. "Vincent, you've done everything but come right out and ask Brynn what she and Tony talked about, and what she's going to do.''

Brynn tried again. "But I—''

"I asked her no such thing. I only said I'd mentioned her to Tony and Michelle. Nothing more.''

"I know you,'' Carla said sternly. "You'll probe and pry until she tells you everything you want to know. Leave her alone, Vinnie.''

"Excuse me?'' Brynn was almost laughing when she finally got their attention. Carla and Vinnie were so funny with their heated fussing, which was so obviously laced with exasperated affection.

When she was certain they were listening to her, she continued, "Michelle and Tony offered me the job, Vinnie. They suggested that I take a little time to think about it before giving them an answer.''

"What's to think about? You need a job—they have one. My grandchildren are sweet natured and very well behaved. Carla and I believe that you will make a good nanny for them. This job was meant for you, Brynn.''

"That's for Brynn to decide for herself, Vincent,'' Carla chided again.

Brynn spoke quickly, before Vinnie felt obliged to defend himself once more. "I just don't want to make a decision too quickly after all that's happened in the past few hours."

"That sounds like a very sensible idea to me," Carla said with a stern look at her husband. "Don't you let this one rush you into anything, *cara*. You do as you think best."

Cara. Brynn didn't speak Italian, but she recognized that word as an endearment. And it warmed her.

Her growing fascination with this family—one member, in particular—was beginning to worry her. Maybe it would be best if she found a job with a large day-care center, rather than taking the job Tony and Michelle had offered. And yet...she had a funny little feeling that Vinnie was right. That Brynn really had been brought to this place at this time for a reason. That she was meant to be nanny to Jason, Carly, Katie and Justin. That her entire life had been forever changed by that one moment of impact on a Dallas highway.

She definitely needed some time to try to think logically before she made any decisions.

Joe found Brynn in Kelly's room late Monday afternoon. It annoyed him greatly that his mouth went dry when he saw her, looking as fresh and pretty as the masses of flowers surrounding her.

He cleared his throat. "Ladies."

They both looked his way in response to the greeting. Kelly spoke first. "Hi, Dr. Joe."

"Looks like a florist shop in here."

She smiled. "The flower arrangements were sent by various members of the Walker and D'Alessandro families. Everyone has been so kind."

He took in the fine lines carved around her mouth, the purple circles beneath her eyes. "I understand you've been in quite a bit of pain today."

She glanced away and tried to speak nonchalantly. "Some. Not too bad."

Because he knew she was lying, and suspected that she was trying to convince everyone—maybe even herself—of her courage and strength, Joe spoke gently. "I'm going to increase your pain medication, Kelly. There's no reason for you to lie here suffering when we have methods available to help you."

Kelly frowned. "I don't want to be doped up. I can't think clearly on medications."

"What's to think about?" Brynn asked practically. "It's not as if you have anything to do at the moment but lie here and heal. You don't have to think all that clearly to do that."

Joe chuckled. "Brynn's exactly right. Let me make you more comfortable."

Kelly sighed. "Whatever you think best, Doc."

"I wish all my patients were so cooperative." Joe glanced at Brynn. "How are *you* holding up? I heard from the grapevine that Dad made you his personal project today."

Brynn smiled then, her eyes warming. "Your father has hauled me around most of Dallas today. He helped me obtain a copy of the police report, and then talk to the insurance agent. He helped me arrange for a rental car, and then he took me to a fabulous Italian restaurant for the best lunch I've eaten in longer than I can remember…"

"Vittorio's?"

She nodded. "Vinnie said it's owned by your relatives. Most of whom I think were there, by the way. He must have introduced me to a dozen people.''

Joe chuckled. ''Only a dozen? That's not 'most' of my family, merely a small sampling.''

She widened her eyes and shook her head. ''I can't even imagine having so many relatives.''

''Sometimes it's great—sometimes it's a pain in the neck,'' he admitted. ''Especially when I've done something stupid or embarrassing and it seems like half of the state of Texas is talking about it the next morning.''

''Do you often do stupid and embarrassing things, Doc?'' Kelly asked with a faint grin.

''Not in years,'' he assured her. ''I haven't dared.''

Brynn glanced at her watch. ''I have to go. I'm having dinner with Tony and Michelle and I'd like to run back to Vinnie and Carla's to change first.''

''You're going to talk to them about the nanny job?'' Kelly asked, looking interested.

Brynn nodded. ''They're going to tell me exactly what they need, and I'm taking them a copy of my résumé and references.''

''Surely Michelle isn't cooking dinner the day she got out of the hospital.''

''She had someone to help her with that this evening,'' Joe interjected.

''I suggested we wait until tomorrow,'' Brynn added. ''I was afraid Michelle wouldn't be up to company this evening. But she insisted she feels fine, and she and Tony want to hire a nanny as soon as possible.''

''If Michelle says she's feeling fine, she is,'' Joe said with a slight shrug. ''She loves nothing more than having people over for dinner.''

Kelly squirmed a bit restlessly in the narrow bed, further evidence of her general discomfort, but she kept her attention on the conversation. "Do you know how to get to their house?" she asked Brynn. "I worry about you driving at night alone in a strange city, especially after…you know."

Brynn nodded gravely. "Tony's picking me up. I told him it wasn't necessary, but he insisted."

"That was very considerate of him."

Brynn rose from the chair in which she'd been sitting. "I really should go. Is there anything else you need now, Kelly?"

"No, thanks."

"I'll leave you to talk to your doctor, then. And you listen to his advice, you hear?"

"Yes, Mom," Kelly murmured ironically.

Brynn looked at Joe. "I suppose I'll be seeing you around," she said, suddenly awkward in a way she had not been with her friend.

"Yes, you will," he replied.

He watched her walk out of the room, and his mouth went dry again as his gaze lingered on the gentle sway of her hips.

Sooner than you think, actually.

Brynn had just finished applying lipstick when there was a light knock on her bedroom door. "Brynn, your ride is here," Carla announced through the wood.

Brynn hurried across the room to open the door, smoothing her loose-fitting red dress and hoping she'd chosen appropriately for the occasion.

Carla seemed to approve. "You look very nice," she said. "That bright red looks so pretty with your dark hair and fair skin."

"Thank you. Um, would you mind checking the tie in the back? I had a little trouble with it."

"Turn around."

Brynn felt a gentle tugging at the back tie that gave the dress its shape, then a pat on her shoulder.

"There you go," Carla said. "It looks fine."

Brynn spun back around, and was surprised to see that Carla's dark eyes had turned a bit misty.

"It's almost like having one of my own in the house again," Carla murmured. "Of course, I had boys, but many's the time I helped them get ready to go out."

And then she laughed softly, a bit self-consciously, and patted Brynn's hand. "Sorry, dear. I was indulging in a moment of nostalgia."

Brynn couldn't help thinking again how lucky Carla's sons were to have had her for a mother.

Brynn wasn't at all prepared for which of those sons waited for her in the living room.

"Joe! Um...*you're* driving me to Tony's?"

He smiled and nodded. "I volunteered. I'm joining you for dinner, then I'll entertain the kids while you talk business with Michelle and Tony."

"You knew this when I saw you at the hospital earlier?"

He nodded.

"And you saw no need to mention it?"

He shrugged, feigning innocence. The expression didn't work very well for him. "It never came up."

Brynn was suddenly nervous in a way that she hadn't been at the mere prospect of having dinner with Michelle and Tony and discussing their job offer. How could she think clearly and logically about a job when all she could concentrate on was how Joe's sexy smile made his dark eyes gleam so appealingly?

This evening wasn't turning out at all the way she had expected.

Chapter Five

Because it seemed the most innocuous topic, Brynn kept the conversation on Kelly's prognosis during the drive.

Joe answered her questions fully and candidly, explaining that it would be weeks before Kelly's right leg would bear her weight, and then only after intensive therapy and with support. He admitted that there was still a danger of infection from bacteria introduced into the open wounds during the time Kelly was trapped in the wreckage, but he assured Brynn that the antibiotics Kelly was taking, along with aggressive monitoring, minimized the risks as much as possible.

"Will she be able to start school in the fall?"

Joe hesitated so long that she was afraid she already knew the answer by the time he spoke.

"Maybe," he said cautiously. "Possibly on crutches.

That's only if everything goes smoothly for the next few weeks, of course.''

She nodded gravely, knowing how much Kelly wanted to begin her graduate work. If it meant getting into school on time, Kelly would cooperate fully with the physical therapy, would probably work hard enough to startle anyone who didn't know her as well as Brynn did.

If there was one word to describe Kelly Morrison, it was tenacious.

Brynn was dazzled into silence when Joe turned the car through the massive stone gates of what appeared to be a near mansion. A spacious, beautifully land-scaped lawn led to a Tudor-style house that looked enormous to Brynn's eyes. She could just see the corner of a trim little brick guest house that sat behind the main house—the one Tony and Michelle had offered her, most likely.

She couldn't even imagine how it would feel to live surrounded by such luxury. She told herself not to be swayed by her initial awe of the place. She'd never craved wealth or extravagance, and she didn't intend to change in that respect now.

She realized that Joe was watching her out of the corner of his eye as he parked in front of the house. Several other vehicles were parked in the spacious driveway, making Brynn wonder exactly how many people were waiting inside. She'd thought the dinner invitation had included just her and Joe.

''This is a lovely home,'' she said, feeling the need for a comment. ''It's, um, big.''

''Yeah. Michelle grew up here. Tony moved in when they married eleven years ago. Apparently, they decided to try to fill it up with kids,'' he added with a grin.

"It must have been filled with children when Michelle was growing up," Brynn commented. "She has so many brothers and sisters."

There was a slight hesitation before Joe replied. "Actually, Michelle was raised as an only child. She and her siblings were orphaned and separated as small children. She was adopted by the couple who owned this house. When her adoptive mother died several years ago, Michelle learned about her brothers and sisters, and started a search for them. They found each other again about the same time Tony and Michelle married."

Brynn was stunned. Michelle seemed so close to her siblings, at least according to the first impression Brynn had received. She remembered now that Michelle had acted oddly when Brynn made a comment about how nice it must have been to grow up with so many siblings to play with. "I didn't know."

Joe shrugged. "They probably would have mentioned it tonight, anyway. Michelle actually met Tony when she hired him to find her family."

Brynn was still thinking about the story of Michelle and her siblings when Joe escorted her to the door and rang the bell. She thought of the kind-eyed, stern-mouthed man who had sat with her during Kelly's surgery. Had Jared been adopted, too, or had he grown up in foster care, as Brynn had? Maybe that explained the immediate bond she'd felt with him that night in the hospital waiting room.

The woman who opened the door looked very much like Michelle, only a few years older. She had the same glossy hair, though hers had more gray threaded through the brown, the same dark-blue eyes, the same warm smile. Perhaps there were a few more lines on her face, but she was still a lovely woman.

"Layla, this is Brynn Larkin," Joe said. "Brynn, meet Michelle's elder sister, Layla Samples."

Brynn held out her hand, only to have Layla cover it with both of hers. "I've heard so much about you," Layla said. "The children have been telling me how nice you are."

Brynn smiled. "The children only met me for a short while."

"Trust me, they form opinions very quickly. And they know who they like."

Joe chuckled. "You must be thinking about Mrs. Webster."

Rueful laughter lighting her eyes, Layla nodded. "Exactly."

"Mrs. Webster?" Brynn repeated curiously.

"A housekeeper Michelle hired a couple of years ago. The little 'angels' took one look at her and instantly disliked her. They ran her off in less than two weeks," Joe explained, his expression wry.

"That doesn't sound like the well-behaved children I met in Michelle's hospital room."

Joe and Layla shared a glance and a smile.

"Let's just say they have a lot of their father in them," Joe murmured.

Brynn wrinkled her nose at Joe. "I don't suppose they have any of their uncle in them?"

He grinned, even as Layla's hands jerked around Brynn's.

Brynn looked questioningly at Layla, who was studying her with a frown.

Layla shook her head, and released Brynn's hand. "Sorry. For a moment, you reminded me of someone. When you wrinkled your nose that way. But I can't…"

"Brynn!" Two little girls in matching pink playsuits pelted through a door and rushed toward Brynn.

She held out her hands to them, a smile spreading across her face. "Carly. Katie. Don't you both look pretty this evening."

Carly patted her dark curls. "Aunt Layla brushed my hair. Mommy was busy with Justin."

Joe cleared his throat loudly. "Excuse me, but have I suddenly become invisible?"

The girls looked at him and dimpled. "Hi, Dr. Joe," they chorused, and then threw themselves at him.

He caught one in each arm, hugging them warmly. "It's about time you noticed I was here."

"We're supposed to talk to company first," Carly lectured him gravely. "Brynn's company. You're fam'ly."

Joe chuckled and ruffled the hair Layla had brushed so neatly. "Is that right?"

Mentally replaying the little girl's words, Brynn thought how much nicer it sounded to be "family" rather than "company."

Layla smiled at Brynn and motioned toward a doorway. "The others are waiting in the den. Shall we?"

Swallowing a sudden nervous lump in her throat, Brynn nodded and followed Layla, aware that Joe and the girls were close at her heels.

There were several people Brynn didn't know in the den. Her fingers locked together in automatic reaction to the wave of nerves that hit her when they all seemed to turn and look at her in unison.

She tried to count faces, telling herself there couldn't possibly be as many people in the room as her over-anxious imagination made it seem. Tony and Michelle were there, of course—Michelle holding court from a chair in the center of the room, Tony standing nearby. A white wicker bassinet rested beside Michelle's chair.

A chubby, pleasant-faced man stood beside a young teenage girl who looked very much like Layla. Husband and daughter? Brynn hazarded.

Four boys sat in one corner of the room, gathered around a board game that apparently required intense concentration. Brynn recognized Jason D'Alessandro, who, at nine, seemed to be the oldest of the group. Two of the boys were probably twins, since they looked almost exactly alike and wore matching shirts and jeans.

The boys weren't the only twins in the room. Two men sat side by side on a couch facing Michelle's chair, looking so much alike Brynn almost questioned her vision. Same light-brown hair, slightly frosted with gray at the temples. Same pale-blue eyes. Same ruggedly attractive, fortyish faces. Same tall, slender, muscular build. Only their expressions were different, one man looking very serious and a bit intimidating, the other smiling broadly and warmly. They stood when she entered, and even their movements were the same.

Two women were the final occupants of the room. A blonde and a brunette of approximately the same ages—late thirties, Brynn would have guessed—they hovered close to the bassinet, the better to admire the sleeping baby inside.

"Brynn." Michelle broke into Brynn's rapid mental assessment of the group. "Come in and meet everyone."

She felt a touch on her shoulder and didn't have to look around to know that it was Joe, and that he was trying to reassure her. Was her attack of shyness so obvious, or was he coming to know her better than she had realized?

Whatever his reason, she appreciated the gesture.

Michelle continued her role as official hostess. "Everyone, this is Brynn Larkin. You've heard us talk about her. Brynn, you've obviously met Layla. This is her husband, Kevin, and their youngest daughter, Brittany." She pointed to the chubby man and the teenage girl, proving Brynn's theory correct as to their identity.

"And this is my brother Ryan Walker, and his wife, Taylor," Michelle continued, pointing to the smiling twin and the brunette, "and my brother Joe Walker, and his wife, Lauren," she added, indicating the serious twin and the blond woman. "The boys with Jason are Joe and Lauren's son, Casey, and Ryan and Taylor's twins, Andrew and Aaron."

Four-year-old Katie seemed to think Brynn needed a bit more clarification. She tugged at Brynn's skirt and pointed to Joe D'Alessandro. "*Dr.* Joe," she said gravely, then turned her chubby finger toward Joe Walker. "*Uncle* Joe."

Joe Walker's formerly serious face creased with a smile, making him look even more like his twin. The other adults chuckled.

Brynn tried to answer as seriously as the tot had spoken. "Thank you, Katie. That will certainly help me keep them apart."

Katie nodded, satisfied that her job was done.

Everyone greeted Brynn politely, and with varying degrees of curiosity. From the way they eyed her, she guessed that Michelle had mentioned she was being considered as a nanny to the D'Alessandro children. She suspected the aunts and uncles were trying to judge her suitability for that position.

"You have the most unusual coloring," the woman who'd been introduced as Taylor Walker mused, studying Brynn's face. "That dark hair and crystal-blue eyes—such an uncommon pairing. Your eyes..."

When Brynn flushed self-consciously, Taylor smiled ruefully and made an apologetic gesture with one slender hand. "Forgive me. I spent several years working as a fashion photographer and now I'm the art director of an advertising agency. I tend to see people in terms of models."

"I think I'll take my family home now before my wife further embarrasses your dinner guest," Ryan said wryly to Michelle, laying his hands on Taylor's shoulders in an affectionate manner that belied his words.

Brynn wasn't sure if he was joking or serious. "You certainly don't have to leave on my account. I'm not embarrassed."

Taylor chuckled. "Ryan's teasing. We weren't planning to stay for dinner, anyway. Joe and Lauren and Ryan and I are taking our boys and Jason to a movie tonight."

At the word "movie," the boys sprang to their feet. "*Space Warriors*. Way cool!" one of them proclaimed.

"I'm sorry I won't be eating with you, Brynn," Jason said, looking a bit conflicted. "But my aunts and uncles invited me to the movie and then we're all going to spend the night at Casey's house..."

"I'm sure you're going to have a wonderful time," Brynn assured him. "You and I will visit another time, okay?"

He smiled up at her. "I'd like that."

"So would I."

Ten minutes later, the two Walker families were gone.

Michelle looked at her remaining family members

and smiled. "Everyone ready to eat? After three days of hospital food, I'm starving."

The dinner was more comfortable than Brynn might have expected. With so many people gathered around the big table in Michelle's dining room, there was rarely a quiet moment for awkwardness to set in.

Carly and Katie, who demanded to sit on either side of Brynn, chattered like magpies throughout the meal. Thirteen-year-old Brittany Samples, while less vociferous, was persuaded by her aunt to talk about the tennis day camp she would be attending during the summer. Joe and Tony carried on what sounded like habitual bickering throughout the meal, exchanging good-natured insults in English interspersed with fluent Italian.

Refusing any assistance, Layla served the excellent meal, which she had prepared on her sister's behalf. She and Michelle talked to Brynn when Carly and Katie gave them a chance, asking questions about Kelly, about Brynn's initial impressions of Dallas and about the work she'd done in the day-care center in Longview.

"I loved the children there," Brynn told them, a lump forming in her throat as she remembered the day she'd had to tell them goodbye. "But I had some differences with the owner of the center. I don't think children should ever be seen as a commodity or their welfare dictated in terms of profit and loss. When she began to serve less nutritious meals and snacks to save money, I spoke up, and that angered her. She didn't want to fire me, because the parents liked me, but she told me in no uncertain terms that I was to do my job and leave the decision making to her."

"Did her budget cuts endanger the children?" Layla asked with a frown.

"No," Brynn admitted. "They were all perfectly legal, within national and state guidelines. They were just...unnecessary. Gloria—my boss—made a good profit off the center. The cuts she made were strictly designed to earn her even more. Little things, like replacing fresh foods with processed ones. Counting ketchup as a vegetable, rather than a condiment. Serving more fried and packaged entrées on the pretext that the children would eat them more readily, when it was my experience that they would eat most of what was served as long as they were hungry and the food was attractively presented."

Layla nodded. "That's what I found when my three children were growing up. Even now that they're teenagers, they will generally choose vegetables and healthy food items when given a choice over fried or packaged selections."

"I like vegetables," Brittany agreed, sticking her fork into a tender, steamed baby carrot. "Of course, I like a burger or pizza every once in a while, too," she added, apparently compelled to be honest.

Brynn smiled. "So do I. The trick is to make them occasional treats, rather than everyday staples. They're much more enjoyable that way, don't you think?"

Brittany returned the smile and nodded, looking pleased that her input to the conversation had been taken seriously. Seeing that Katie and Carly had finished their desserts and were beginning to get restless, she volunteered to take them into another room to play. They accepted eagerly, dragging her off to admire their toys. The adults lingered at the table over coffee, while baby Justin slept peacefully in the bassinet Tony had carried into the room for him.

"You said you're working toward a degree in elementary education, Brynn?" Layla asked, encouraging her to converse with them more.

Brynn nodded. "I like children," she said simply. "And I'm good at it. On the rare occasions when we'd get very young children in the foster home where I lived, I was always the one who seemed to take care of them."

There was a moment of silence and then Layla asked, "Did you live in only one foster home?"

Her eyes on her nearly empty plate, Brynn shook her head. "Several. But only one from the time I was thirteen until I graduated high school at eighteen."

"And were you happy there?"

"Reasonably."

Layla nodded, accepting Brynn's guarded answer at face value. "I spent most of my childhood in a foster home, as well," she said. "Our parents died when I was only ten, and no one wanted to take seven children, so we were split up. I was fortunate to be placed into a very good foster home, where I was able to remain until I was on my own. Very kind people, who treated me as their own daughter. Michelle and Lindsay, our youngest sister, were adopted by different families, and both were very close to their adoptive parents. The boys weren't as lucky. Their foster experiences were unsuccessful. Jared was eleven when we were separated, and was never able to form bonds with his foster families. The twins were so unhappy they ran away at sixteen and have been on their own ever since. Miles was placed in so many different homes and institutions that he probably never felt truly at home."

"Miles?" Brynn frowned, trying to remember faces to go with all the names. She hadn't met Lindsay, and didn't even remember hearing the name Miles before. In fact, she would have sworn that Michelle had said there were only six siblings, not seven.

"Miles died young," Michelle said sadly. "Before the rest of us were reunited. I never had a chance to meet him. I was so young when our parents died that I have no memory of the time we all lived together."

"But you have each other now," Brynn mused, thinking that the sad story had a happy ending after all. "From what I've seen, you've become close."

Michelle and Layla exchanged somewhat misty smiles.

"Yes," Michelle murmured, "very close."

"We've been blessed," Layla agreed.

"It's really amazing that you were able to find everyone. I know a few people who have been looking for their birth families for years," Brynn murmured.

Michelle turned her proud smile in her husband's direction. "We had an excellent investigator on our case."

Tony deflected the lovingly given compliment. "It's gotten a lot easier since computers have become so common. Reunions of biological family members are becoming almost commonplace."

Brynn nodded thoughtfully. "I've seen many stories in the newspapers and on television about reunited families lately. One that particularly interested me rather recently was the story of two brothers who actually worked at the same company and became close friends before they discovered they had the same birth parents. It seemed like such a bizarre coincidence."

"It happens frequently," Tony repeated. "Although

not all the reunions are as happy or successful as Michelle's have been.''

"Do you have any brothers or sisters, Brynn?" Kevin asked.

"No. My mother told me that my father died before I was born. He had no other children, and neither did my mother, who died when I was thirteen.''

"And what about other family?" Layla wanted to know. "There was no one to take you in when your mother passed away?''

Knowing Layla was remembering her own circumstances, Brynn shook her head. "My parents met in an institution for orphaned teenagers. Neither had families. They hadn't been on their own very long when my father died in an accident. My mother raised me on her own, for as long as she was able. When she became…ill…she had no choice but to place me in foster care. I lived in several homes when I was very young, leaving each when my mother felt well enough to care for me. And then she…died when I was thirteen, and I went into the home I told you about. The same one Kelly moved into a couple of years later, when her own single mother was diagnosed with cancer. We've thought of ourselves as sisters ever since.''

If the others noticed the hesitations in Brynn's story, they didn't comment.

"As our sister Lindsay, who adores her adoptive family, can testify, not all family relationships are formed by blood,'' Layla murmured.

It was nice to be among people who truly understood, Brynn mused.

Matter-of-factly, Layla began to gather dirty dishes. "I'm going to clean the kitchen now. Michelle, why don't you and Tony take Brynn into the den, where you can talk.''

"Oh, let me help you with the dishes." Brynn sprang to her feet, both eager to help and wanting to stall that talk.

Kevin snatched up a bowl before Brynn could touch it. "No problem. I'll help her."

"So will I," said Joe, gathering silverware. "We're quite capable of taking care of this. Go talk with Tony and Michelle."

Brynn gave in gracefully and followed her hosts to their den.

It was nearly nine by the time the evening came to an end. Brynn, who had been holding little Justin, handed the baby back to his mother and moved toward the door with Joe.

"We'll talk more soon," Michelle assured Brynn, seeing them off with a smile.

"Yes. Thank you again for inviting me for dinner. I really enjoyed the evening."

Tony punched Joe's shoulder. "See you, *fratello*—next time you beg a free meal out of us, most likely."

Joe grinned. "I'm going to take any chance I get for a home-cooked meal. Why d'you think I spend so much time with you married guys?"

"Because it's easier than learning to cook for yourself, I suppose."

"*Esattamente*. Exactly," he translated when Brynn looked at him with a lifted eyebrow.

Back at his car, Joe opened the passenger door for Brynn. "Watch your dress," he warned as he prepared to close the door after she'd gotten in.

She lifted the length of red fabric out of the doorway

and then fastened her seat belt as Joe closed her door, walked around the front of the vehicle and slid behind the wheel. She watched while Joe snapped his own belt and started the engine. "You and Tony are very close, aren't you?"

He shrugged, guiding the car out of the driveway. "I suppose. I don't stop to analyze our relationship very often."

Brynn hoped he didn't take his family for granted. He was so lucky to have them. "You speak Italian a lot with your family."

"Habit. It was important to our grandparents that we learn the language, so we used it quite a bit in our home."

"It's a beautiful language. I always wanted to learn Italian. Maybe I'll take a class someday."

"It's not so hard to learn. The pronunciation rules actually make more sense than English."

"Most languages do, I think," Brynn replied with a smile. "Kelly's mother was from Germany, and Kelly speaks a little German. I took the required two years of Spanish in high school, but I remember just enough to order eggs for breakfast—badly."

"Tony's teaching his kids Italian. Maybe they'll share what they know with you. You *are* going to take the nanny job, aren't you?"

He'd slid the question so smoothly into the conversation that Brynn had to smile at his skill at prying without seeming to. He was much better at it than his father, she reflected.

"Maybe. I've asked Tony to check the references I gave him, just so we'll all know proper procedures were followed. I've given them a copy of my résumé. He and

Michelle explained very thoroughly what the job would entail.''

"Sounds like you're being totally professional about it.''

The slight hint of amusement in Joe's comment put Brynn on the defensive. "Being responsible for children is an important job. I want Michelle and Tony to be fully confident they've hired the right person.''

The crease in Joe's right cheek deepened. "I'm only teasing a bit about there being any doubt you're perfect for the job. You have experience, training and impressive credentials. The kids like you. Tony and Michelle like you. Mom and Dad like you. *I* like you. Why wouldn't you be the right person?''

For some reason, Brynn's heart fluttered when Joe said he liked her. Feeling sheepishly like a smitten adolescent, she cleared her throat and tried to concentrate on the real conversation. "I'll still feel better about their offer after they've verified my qualifications.''

"And when they've done that and renewed their job offer—as I'm sure they will—will you accept?''

Brynn tucked a strand of hair behind her ear. "Probably.''

It sounded like too good an offer to refuse. She would have time to spend with Kelly during her recuperation, evenings free to take classes once Kelly was back on her feet and in school, and even a place to live. Michelle and Tony had repeated their offer of the guest house and their reassurances that Kelly was welcome to live there, too.

"They're being unbelievably generous, especially considering the fact that I'm basically a stranger to them.''

Joe slanted her a smile that made her heart jerk again.

"You aren't a stranger anymore, Brynn. You're a friend. I think we all feel that way."

She bit her lip. "I don't know what to say. Everything has happened so quickly. Everyone in your family has just opened their arms to me."

"You're forgetting we're a family that grew very quickly within a short time. In less than two years, Michelle went from a single woman raised as an only child to a married woman with five siblings, dozens of in-laws and a whole litter of nieces and nephews. Relationships develop quickly within the Walker and D'Alessandro clans."

Brynn laced her fingers in her lap and moistened her lips. "I, on the other hand, have been on my own—except for Kelly—for a long time. It takes me a bit longer to adjust to sweeping changes. I was just getting accustomed to the idea of living in a new city and finding a new job. Now I have all these other circumstances and opportunities to deal with. Frankly, my head is spinning."

Joe's smile turned sympathetic. He reached across the console to cover her hands with his, and gave a friendly squeeze. "When you put it that way, I can understand how you must be feeling. Don't let any of us rush you into making decisions, Brynn. You take all the time you need."

She'd thought her head was spinning before. Now, with Joe's hand holding hers, she felt positively dizzy. She was glad she was sitting.

"Will you—" She stopped to clear her throat. "Will you be checking on Kelly again this evening?"

He put his hand back on the steering wheel. "I will if you'd like me to. In fact, why don't we both check on her. We can stop by the hospital for a few minutes before I take you home.''

She told herself she was glad he'd pulled his hand away, even though her own suddenly felt cold. ''Yes, I'd like that.''

Joe nodded and signaled for a turn. They spent the rest of the short drive to the hospital talking about Kelly again. Doctor to friend of patient.

Brynn found that much more comfortable than the more intimate friendship Joe had described moments earlier.

After a short visit with Kelly, Joe drove Brynn to his parents' home and walked her to the door. ''I'm not coming in,'' he said. ''I have an early surgery in the morning.''

''Thank you for driving me this evening. It was very thoughtful of you.''

A chuckle escaped him as he reached out to brush a hair from her cheek. ''Always so prim. Has anyone ever nicknamed you Mary Poppins?''

Brynn frowned. She wasn't sure if Joe was complimenting her or gently insulting her.

His chuckle turned to a low laugh. ''Want your first Italian lesson? Repeat after me... *Via al diavolo.*''

''*Via al diavolo,*'' she repeated obediently. ''What did I say?''

''You told me to go to hell,'' he replied cheerfully.

''Joe!''

''Hey, if you want to learn the language, you might as well learn something more useful than how to order eggs for breakfast.''

She put her hand on the doorknob. ''Good night, Joe.''

''*Buona notte,* Brynn.''

She had the odd feeling that he lingered a moment outside the door after she closed herself inside. Just as she stood there in the entryway for a while, looking at that door and picturing him on the other side.

It was only when she heard the sound of his car starting that she was able to turn and walk toward her temporary bedroom.

Chapter Six

Three days later, on Thursday, Brynn moved into the guest house to begin her new career as nanny to the four young D'Alessandro children.

She had plenty of assistance for her move. Tony and young Jason, Jared and Shane cheerfully loaded boxes into the back of Jared's pickup while Vinnie barked orders and frequently got in the way.

The guest house was beautifully furnished. Even though it hadn't been occupied in several years, it had been well maintained, and Michelle and Tony had arranged for it to be cleaned and aired before Brynn moved in. Fresh flowers in glass vases had been placed in nearly every room. Brynn, who loved flowers but rarely splurged to buy any for herself, found that the most touching gesture of all.

Brynn's eager helpers even insisted on helping her unpack the linens, small kitchen utensils, books and knickknacks that were the sum of Brynn's and Kelly's belongings, outside of their clothes. There wasn't a lot of unpacking to do, since both Brynn and Kelly had gotten rid of everything unnecessary to facilitate the move. They had brought only what had fit into the roomy trunk of Brynn's little car, and piled to the top in the back seat.

Jared's wife, Cassie, and ten-year-old daughter, Molly, both vivacious and talkative redheads, joined them for a late lunch. After the past few days, Brynn was no longer surprised when members of this family greeted her like a long-lost pal. Cassie was no exception. By the time they'd finished lunch, Brynn had heard the story of how Cassie and Jared had met when Cassie, then an operative of Tony's investigation firm, had tracked Jared down and cajoled him into being reunited with his siblings. Only months after finding Jared, Cassie had married him.

"Finder's keepers," she boasted, patting her husband's tanned, firm cheek.

"Everyone knows you married him so you could have me for a stepson," Shane taunted, taking advantage of a lull when Cassie stopped talking.

"And me for a daughter," Molly piped in, not to be left out.

"And me for a brother-in-law, rather than a boss," Tony remarked with a half grin.

"What am I?" Katie asked, frowning.

"My niece," Cassie replied.

"And what's Brynn?"

Everyone at the table smiled at Brynn.

"A friend." Jared spoke up for the first time.

Brynn's smile felt a bit tremulous when she smiled at him across the table. "Thank you."

Jared shrugged, typically uncomfortable with sentiment. "What's for dessert?" he asked his sister rather abruptly.

Michelle stood. "Your favorite. Fresh strawberry cake. And now I'm glad I made it for you," she added, leaning over to kiss his cheek as she passed him toward the kitchen.

Cassie jumped to her feet. "I'll help you serve."

"So will I," Brynn said, rising to start gathering dishes.

She was becoming more convinced by the hour that she'd made the right decision when she'd accepted the position as nanny to the D'Alessandro children.

Knowing Brynn had moved into the guest house that day, Joe thought it would be a nice gesture to surprise her with a housewarming gift on his way home from work Thursday. But he was the one surprised when he entered the open front door of the guest house to find Brynn sitting on Shane Walker's broad shoulders, both of them laughing and looking perfectly comfortable in their unusual position.

Shane stood in the middle of the guest-house living room, directly beneath the nine-foot peak of the cathedral ceiling. Balanced on his shoulders, steadied by Shane's hands on her blue-jeaned thighs, Brynn was changing a bulb in the ceiling-fan light fixture above her head.

Joe was reluctantly aware that they made a nice-looking couple. They were both young, fit and undeniably attractive. Both unattached. Joe could think of no good reason they shouldn't flirt and enjoy each other's company.

Which didn't mean he had to like it.

Shane spotted Joe first. Seeming to find it a common occurrence to be found with a woman on his shoulders, Shane nodded affably. "Hey, Doc. How's it going?"

Brynn gasped and swayed, causing Shane to have to tighten his grip on her legs.

"Careful up there," he warned.

"Have you ever heard of using a stepladder?" Joe asked, sounding more cross than he'd intended.

"Couldn't find one," Shane replied flippantly.

Joe lifted an eyebrow. "Did you look?"

Shane's mischievous chuckle was his only answer.

"I'm, um, finished up here," Brynn said, giving the bulb a final twist.

It bothered Joe that Brynn had stopped laughing when he came in. He set the wrapped gift he'd carried in on a table and reached up to steady her with a hand at either side of her waist while Shane knelt carefully to allow Brynn to disembark.

Joe was reluctant to release her even when Brynn was steady on her feet again. She felt too darned good between his hands.

She settled the issue by stepping quickly out of his reach. "I wasn't expecting you this evening."

"I thought I'd stop by and see if you needed any help with anything." He looked around the room, which was as neat as a pin. "I see you've got everything under control."

"Yes. I've had a lot of assistance today. Michelle and Tony even stocked the pantry and refrigerator for me. Would you like a soda?"

"No, thank you."

Shane nodded toward the coffee table. "Looks like you brought a present. I don't suppose it's for me."

Joe gave the younger man a look. "It's for Brynn. A housewarming gift."

Brynn looked from Joe to the package and back again. "That was very nice of you."

"Aren't you going to open it?" Shane prodded when she made no move toward the gift.

"Yes, of course." Somewhat tentatively, Brynn lifted the package. "It's heavy."

Increasingly self conscious, Joe watched as she peeled away the cheerful, buttercup-yellow paper a helpful salesclerk had selected for him. He wondered now if he'd made the right choice of gift. It was something he'd seen in the window of a gift shop near his office. No designer name on it, or anything like that, but it was a pretty little bauble and he'd thought she might like it—but maybe he'd been wrong.

He felt himself begin to relax when Brynn opened the box and gasped in obvious pleasure.

"A crystal clock! Joe, this is lovely. Thank you."

He smiled. "You're welcome."

"Hey, that *is* nice," Shane commented, studying the intricately cut crystal as Brynn set the clock carefully on a shelf of a sparsely filled bookcase built into one wall of the living room.

Joe shrugged. "Just something I saw in a window." He changed the subject abruptly. "What do you think of this place, Brynn? Think you'll be comfortable here?"

"How could I not be? It's such a nice little house."

It had been a long time since Joe had been in the guest house—since right after Betty and Arthur, the former inhabitants, had moved out six or seven years ago. He glanced around, remembering that the place consisted of this nice-sized living room, an eat-in kitchen, two bedrooms and a shared bath. Small, but practical.

"When do you start your nanny duties?"

"Michelle and I are going to meet tomorrow morning to work out a schedule. Beginning next Monday, she wants to spend a couple of hours a week concentrating on her work, which she says she can do in her home office while the baby sleeps. I'll take care of the other three children to give her time to concentrate."

Joe nodded, not at all surprised that Michelle was already eager to get back to her duties as charity administrator for the large, wealthy corporation founded by her late adoptive father. Michelle took those responsibilities very seriously, and had done an admirable job of juggling work and family during the past ten or eleven years. Having been raised by a working mother, Joe knew what a delicate balancing act that could be.

Of course, it didn't hurt that Michelle could afford to hire the best help, he thought, glancing at Brynn. He was well aware that many working mothers didn't have that option.

Shane looked at his watch, drawing Joe's attention to him. Joe supposed he should leave. After all, he'd delivered the gift and reassured himself that Brynn had everything under control. There was no reason for him to stay any longer. Brynn and Shane probably had plans for the evening. He should leave them alone.

Why was he so damned reluctant to do so?

But it was Shane who said, "I'd better be going. I have some paperwork to catch up on this evening. Is there anything else I can do before I leave, Brynn?"

"No, I can't think of anything else. Thank you so much for all you've done today, Shane."

He ruffled her already disheveled hair, the gesture as

casual and affectionate as if they'd known each other for years. "You've got my number if you need anything else."

She smiled and nodded, while smoothing her hair with one hand.

"See ya, Doc." Shane sketched a salute as he passed Joe on the way to the door.

"Yeah. Later, Shane." Should he leave, too? Even if he didn't want to quite yet?

No, he decided as the front door closed behind Shane, leaving Joe alone with Brynn. Maybe he'd stay a little while longer.

Brynn smoothed her hands down the sides of her jeans and cleared her throat, suddenly nervous now that she and Joe were alone. After a day of moving and unpacking, she had to look a mess. Her hair had been rumpled even before Shane had made it worse, her jeans and T-shirt were wrinkled and smudged and what little makeup she'd applied that morning had long since worn away.

Eyeing Joe's perfectly tailored gray jacket, crisp pale-blue shirt, sharply pleated charcoal slacks and neatly knotted silk tie, she wondered how he could look so fresh after a long day at work. Not that Joe could look bad, no matter what the condition of his clothing, she thought wryly.

She glanced again at the pretty little crystal clock on the bookshelf. She was incredibly touched that Joe had thought to bring it…too much so, perhaps. She had to be careful not to read too much into the gesture. The gift meant no more than all the assistance Shane had given her during the day, and she had read no more into that than an offer of friendship.

What more could there be between her and Dr. Joe D'Alessandro?

She slid her fingertips into her jeans pockets. "Are you sure I can't get you something to drink? Cola, tea, coffee?"

He looked at his watch. "It's getting close to dinnertime. I don't suppose you've eaten."

She shook her head. "I was just going to make some soup or something quick tonight. Michelle invited me to join them, but I don't want her to think I expect them to include me in all the family meals. I have a very nice kitchen here, and I'm quite capable of feeding myself."

"I'm sure you are. However, I'm starving, and I'm a lousy cook. How about going out for a bite to eat with me?"

"I, er...out?" she repeated stupidly.

He smiled. "Out. As in restaurant? And then we could stop by the hospital for a little while, if you'd like."

She had had every intention of visiting Kelly that evening. She'd expected to do so alone. "Surely you don't want to go back to the hospital again this evening. For you, it must be like going back to the office after dinner."

He shrugged. "I practically live there, anyway. Besides, I have another patient I'd like to look in on this evening. A twelve-year-old boy whose arm was crushed in a farming accident yesterday. He isn't doing very well. There's a strong chance he'll lose the arm."

"The poor boy. I hope you can save his arm."

"I'm doing my best," Joe replied a bit grimly. "So, since I'm going to the hospital, anyway, and since you and I both have to eat, we might as well go together, don't you think?"

There were probably several reasons she should decline. Brynn simply couldn't think of any at the moment. "I'll need to change."

Joe nodded. "Take your time. I haven't had a chance to sit down all day. I'll just sit in here and catch up on the news while you change."

Proving he'd been in the guest house before, he crossed the living room, opened a cabinet door built into the bookcase unit that made up one wall and revealed the television stored inside. Brynn hadn't known about that set herself, until she'd discovered it by accident only a short while earlier.

It gave her a funny feeling to see Joe making himself so comfortable in her new home. Maybe because it felt a little too right to have him here.

She turned and headed for the bedroom she'd chosen as her own, telling herself she would use the time while she changed to remind herself how foolish it was for her to start fantasizing about things that were never meant to be.

Not being in the mood to share Brynn with a couple dozen family members, Joe didn't even consider taking her to Vittorio's. He chose, instead, a nice, anonymous chain restaurant where he knew he could get a fairly decent steak.

He watched across the small, candlelit table as Brynn placed her order for grilled chicken. The smile she gave the young waiter made the kid's Adam's apple bob in his skinny throat.

Funny thing was, Brynn seemed to have no idea just how attractive she was. Maybe it was because she'd had so many other things on her mind during the few days he'd known her—but he didn't think so. She simply seemed to have no concept of what big, crystal-blue eyes, a delicately boned, heart-shaped face and a soft, vulnerable mouth could do to a man.

He looked quickly down at the salad that had just been served to him and jabbed his fork into a carrot with more force than strictly necessary. "So you had plenty of help with your move?" he asked, reluctantly remembering how she'd looked perched so cheerfully on Shane Walker's shoulders.

Brynn chuckled. "Plenty. Your father barked orders, Tony argued with him about the best way to do everything, Shane and Jason roughhoused, while Jared quietly loaded all the boxes onto his truck."

Joe grinned. "I could have described that scene without even being there."

As though suddenly concerned that he might have misread her comments as criticisms, Brynn spoke quickly. "Actually, they were all a great deal of help. I appreciated everything they did for me."

"They're a great bunch. Exhausting at times, but well-intentioned."

"They're wonderful. I still can't get over how lucky Kelly and I are that you and Michael were nearby when we had our accident."

Joe stuffed his mouth with salad to avoid having to come up with an answer to that.

Brynn's expression turned pensive, as it usually did when she spoke of the accident. "Joe... is there any chance Kelly could lose her leg?"

She must be thinking about the boy he'd mentioned earlier. "We talked about this a little, Brynn, remember? There's little chance that she could lose the leg. We've been treating her very aggressively against the infections that could cause that. As I've mentioned, I'm more concerned now with making sure her leg won't be significantly shortened. If she continues to do as well as she has so far, I'll take her back into surgery next week.''

Expecting another question about Kelly, he was a bit surprised when Brynn took the conversation into a slightly different direction.

"Have you always wanted to be a doctor?"

"Not until my junior year of high school. Before that, I always assumed I'd go into law, like Mom and Michael, or follow Dad and Tony into the police academy.''

"What made you change your mind?"

"I broke my arm riding a friend's motorcycle. Falling off a friend's motorcycle, to be more precise. It was a pretty bad break, and it required an orthopedic surgeon's care. By the time the bones had set, I knew I'd found what I wanted to do. I considered specializing in sports medicine for a while, but I really like the challenge and variety of what I do now.''

"You must have worked very hard to get where you are. Surgery requires a lot of education, doesn't it?"

"Seems like I've been in school most of my life," he admitted ruefully. "I've only been in practice on my own for a couple of years.''

"It must have been difficult to remain so dedicated for such a long time.''

He shrugged. "There was nothing else I wanted to do.''

He was trying to think of something else to say, when a musically feminine voice spoke his name.

"Joe D'Alessandro. Goodness, it seems like forever since I've seen you. Where've you been hiding yourself, hmm?''

Joe looked up to find an attractive, auburn-haired woman standing beside his table, a touch of reproach in the polished smile she gave him. He almost squirmed, remembering that he'd promised to call her after their last date but never had. It wasn't like him to be so ill-mannered. He didn't suppose it would make her feel better if he admitted that she hadn't even crossed his mind since the last time he'd seen her.

"I've been busy," he said, instead, knowing the lame excuse was little better than the truth. "Um, Brynn Larkin, this is Aubrey Carpenter. Dr. Aubrey Carpenter," he added, remembering that such distinctions were important to Aubrey.

Which was one of the reasons he hadn't called her, most likely.

Brynn murmured a response.

Aubrey said something in return, then turned dismissively away from Brynn and back to Joe. "Call me?"

"I, uh, I'll probably be seeing you around," he said instead.

Her eyes darkened, but Aubrey's chin stayed high. "Yes, of course. Goodbye, Joe."

She walked gracefully away, leaving him feeling somewhat below a slug on the natural food chain. Which really wasn't fair, considering that he hadn't been the one who'd tried to turn a couple of innocuous dinner dates into something a lot more meaningful.

He glanced across the table again. Brynn was concentrating studiously on her dinner, her expression hidden from him. Joe cleared his throat and stabbed his fork into his steak.

The visit with Kelly was short but pleasant. While Joe was gone, checking on his other patients, Brynn sat beside Kelly's bed, making her laugh with anecdotes about the move and her enthusiastic helpers.

"I can't wait to meet them all," Kelly murmured. "And to see your new place."

"Our new place," Brynn corrected her. "Michelle and Tony said you're welcome to stay there with me as long as you need to. There are two bedrooms, and plenty of room for the two of us. I start work tomorrow, and I'll be busy during the days, but I'm off evenings and weekends unless Michelle and Tony need me to watch the children while they go out."

"So, basically, you're an on-call nanny."

"Basically, yes," Brynn agreed with a smile. "And I think it's going to work out beautifully."

"I'm glad. Did I understand that you had dinner with Joe before coming here tonight?"

Brynn tried to answer in the same light, casual tone with which she'd spoken of the others she'd spent time with that day. "Yes, we stopped by a restaurant on the way. He was hungry."

"You've been spending a lot of time with him, haven't you?"

"No more than any of the others," Brynn answered a bit too quickly. "He's—they've all been very kind."

"Mmm. Seems like I've been picking up some vibes between the two of you. You suppose it's the medication?"

Frowning at her friend's teasing, Brynn spoke firmly. "Either that or a seriously overactive imagination. There's nothing going on between me and your doctor, Kelly."

"Maybe there could be, if you'd make a little effort for a change."

"Don't be ridiculous."

Kelly hadn't seen Aubrey Carpenter, Brynn thought glumly. *Dr.* Aubrey Carpenter, she corrected herself. Beautiful, sophisticated, glamorous, highly educated Dr Aubrey Carpenter, who obviously had a history with Joe, unsatisfying as it had obviously been on her part. As far as Brynn was concerned, it couldn't have been more clear how far out of Joe's league she was, at least when it came to dating.

Not that their quick dinner together had even resembled a date, she assured herself flatly.

Kelly shifted in the bed, then grimaced.

"Are you all right?"

"Chill out, Brynn, I'm fine. Just really tired of this bed. I'd like to be starting my new life in Dallas, too— and lying in a hospital bed isn't what I had in mind."

Brynn started to speak, but Kelly stopped her with a sigh and a shake of her head.

"I'm sorry. I didn't mean to complain."

"God knows you have a right to," Brynn assured her, her voice tremulous. "You say whatever you want to me, Kelly, okay? You don't have to be strong and cheerful all the time. You can complain or curse or groan or whine with me, and I'll never think less of you. *Capisce?*"

Kelly's frown turned to a giggle. "'*Capisce?*' Could be you've been hanging around Italians too long, Brynn."

"Could be," Brynn answered, pleased that she'd drawn a smile from her friend. Even as she tried to return it, she couldn't help wondering if there was a grain of truth in Kelly's words.

Joe insisted on walking Brynn to her door, even though she pointed out that the guest house was located on the D'Alessandros' very secure estate. She wondered if he expected her to invite him in. And what, if anything, he expected after that.

She turned to him at the door. "Thank you for dinner."

He nodded, making no move to step toward the threshold. "You'll be comfortable here tonight?"

"Yes, very. Tony showed me where all the security alarms are. I have no doubt that I'll be safe here."

"If you need anything..."

"There are any number of people I can call," she assured him. "Your mother made a list of telephone numbers for me...everyone in your family and Michelle's, I think."

"Is my number on the list?"

"Yes."

"Good. Don't hesitate to use it."

She couldn't imagine why she would need to call Joe, but she nodded anyway. "Thank you."

"You're probably tired. You should go on in and get some rest. I'll talk to you later."

She nodded. "Good night, Joe."

As if by impulse, he reached out to touch her cheek with his fingertips. "Good night, Brynn. Sleep well."

And then he turned on one heel and walked away.

Brynn closed herself inside her new home and stood for a moment in the living room, adjusting to the strangeness of her surroundings. And then she realized that she had her hand on her cheek, just over the spot where Joe had touched her. That fleeting touch had felt almost as intimate as a kiss, and had shaken her more than she wanted to admit.

She couldn't help wondering what it would have been like if Joe *had* kissed her.

Chapter Seven

The Friday-morning meeting with Michelle was conducted in a professional manner that Brynn appreciated. There was no hint of charity; Michelle was the one who needed assistance, and Brynn was in a position to fill that need. They were employer and new employee, polite, friendly but aware of each other's boundaries. Brynn left that meeting even more reassured that she'd made the right decision, and she believed Michelle felt the same way. All in all, it was a very productive session.

Brynn spent the weekend settling into her new quarters and getting acquainted with her charges. Officially, her job wouldn't begin until Monday, but she wanted the children to be completely comfortable with her by the time she became responsible for their safety and behavior during her shifts.

They spent Saturday afternoon playing in the beautiful backyard, which had been transformed into a children's paradise. A big wooden jungle gym held swings, a slide, gymnastic rings, an airplane-shaped glider and a lookout tower with small round windows and a fireman's pole. There was also a sandbox, a picnic table and a shaded lawn swing that seemed perfectly suited for a peaceful interlude with a good book.

By the end of the afternoon, Brynn had gotten to know the children well enough to realize that they were very different individuals. Nine-year-old Jason was the quiet one, bright and introspective, even tempered and easygoing, but with a slightly mischievous sense of humor that Brynn found enchanting. Six-year-old Carly was the instigator, impulsive, inventive, stubborn and a bit temperamental, but irresistible when she turned on that D'Alessandro charm. Little Katie was a four-year-old heartbreaker, loving, demonstrative, curious, happy. Her musical giggle was so contagious that Brynn spent much of the afternoon laughing—something she hadn't done enough lately.

It was a thoroughly delightful day.

Tony found them late that afternoon all snuggled together on the lawn swing. Jason and Carly sat on either side of Brynn, who held Katie in her lap while reading aloud from a book of animal stories.

"This looks cozy."

Carly glanced up from the pictures in the book when her father spoke. "Hi, Daddy. Brynn's reading to us. Sorry, there's no room for you on the swing."

"That's okay. I hear you've been out here all afternoon. Been having a good time?"

Carly nodded enthusiastically. "We've been telling Brynn all about us."

Brynn smiled. "Nothing too personal," she assured

her employer. "I've been hearing about school and friends and soccer games and dance lessons."

Tony chuckled. "Your ears are probably tired. I'm sure you're ready for a break. Go wash up, guys, we're going to Paul and Teresa's house for dinner."

"But I want to hear the end of the story," Katie protested.

Brynn carefully placed a bookmark between the pages. "We'll finish it later," she promised. "I won't forget where we left off."

Jason climbed off the swing, then turned back to Brynn. "Are you coming with us tonight?"

Michelle had invited Brynn to join them at Tony's cousin's house for dinner, but Brynn had politely declined. Now was the time to make it clear that she had a life of her own after working hours. Or, at least, she hoped to make a life of her own, eventually. "No, Jason. I have other plans for the evening."

"What are you going to do?" Katie wanted to know.

"That," her father said, lifting the child onto his hip, "is none of our business. Brynn, you'll let us know if you need anything?"

"Of course. Have a nice time, everyone. I'll see you later, okay?"

"'Bye, Brynn."

"'Bye, Carly."

"'Bye, Brynn. Don't lose the book."

"I won't lose the book, Katie."

Jason lingered a moment after his father headed toward the house with the girls. "You're sure you'll be okay by yourself?"

Both touched and exasperated by his concern—another protective D'Alessandro male, she couldn't help thinking—Brynn put his hand on his shoulder. "I'll be fine, Jason. I'm a grown-up, remember?"

He nodded. "Okay. Well...have fun."

"Thank you." She couldn't help smiling as she watched him hurry after his family. And then she walked toward the guest house, where she planned to shower and change for her own plans for the evening— a nice, long visit with Kelly at the hospital.

It was probably because Joe wanted to see Brynn so badly that he carefully avoided her for several days. He needed to distance himself from her, decide what it was about her that kept her in his mind.

By Wednesday, he still hadn't pinned down the reason. He only knew he hadn't stopped thinking about her for more than an hour or so at a time since he'd left her on her doorstep last Thursday evening.

As he drove through the open gates of his brother's home Wednesday evening, he told himself his reason for being there was simply to visit his family and make sure all was going well with Brynn as the new nanny. After all, he felt some measure of responsibility for her being there. He was the one who'd asked his friends and family to watch out for her during those first traumatic hours after the accident.

Bull. He was here because he wanted to see Brynn, he acknowledged grimly as he parked in front of the main house. Even if it was only to find out whether nearly a week's absence had changed anything about the unsettling way he'd always reacted to her.

Though he was tempted to head straight for the guest house, something made him climb the steps to the main house, instead. Cowardice, most likely, he thought as he jabbed a finger at the doorbell.

Michelle opened the door. "Hi, Joe," she said, accustomed to her husband's family's drop-by visits.

He kissed her cheek. "You're looking good. How are you feeling?"

"Almost back to normal. It feels so good to see my feet again." Her smile was a bit rueful as she patted her shrinking stomach. "You look tired. Rough day?"

He'd had to watch a twelve-year-old boy deal with the loss of an arm. There was nothing Joe hated worse than admitting defeat. "Long day," he summed it up. "Is Tony home?"

"He's in the den. Come on in."

It always lifted Joe's spirits to see his big brother. He'd visit with Joe for a while before finding Brynn, he decided.

But when he entered the den, his careful planning fell apart.

Brynn stood in the center of the room, delicately beautiful in a pale-pink top with one of the flowing, flowered skirts she favored. Little Justin lay in her arms, gazing at her in intense, infant concentration as she cooed to him with a look of utter infatuation on her face.

Joe's mind went blank, his tongue numb. He couldn't have spoken had he tried at that moment.

As if suddenly sensing his presence, Brynn looked up. Her eyes widened, then locked with Joe's. Something arced between them that Joe didn't think he'd imagined. He couldn't have said how much time passed while they stood there, staring at each other, but it couldn't have been long since Tony didn't seem to notice anything unusual.

"Hey, Joe. How's it going?"

With some difficulty that he hoped wasn't apparent to the others, Joe found his voice. "Okay. You?"

"Pretty good. We wrapped up that insurance case I was telling you about on the phone yesterday."

Joe dragged his gaze from Brynn to his brother. "Did it turn out the way you'd expected?"

"Yeah. The guy was trying to run a scam. Said he'd been robbed. Turned out he'd pawned the stuff himself under a fake name, then filed a bogus police report and insurance claim."

"But you knew the truth all along."

"Ryan did. Insurance fraud is his specialty."

Joe found himself turning to Brynn again. "How are you?"

"Fine, thank you." Her response was just a bit too prim to sound entirely natural.

"The little monsters haven't run you off yet, hmm?"

She laughed, seeming to relax a little. "Don't talk that way about my little angels."

"Man, have they got *you* fooled."

As if they'd been summoned by the insinuation against them, the children burst into the room just then. The girls squealed in delight, and launched themselves at "Dr. Joe." Jason greeted his uncle with only slightly more restrained enthusiasm.

Joe spent the next few minutes trying to follow three separate conversations as his nephew and nieces all talked at once, telling him everything they'd done since the last time he'd seen them. And even as he took in nearly everything they said, part of his concentration remained on Brynn, and how he'd felt when he'd walked in to see her holding his infant nephew in her arms.

Tony spoke loudly enough to be heard over his children's chattering. "Want something to drink, Joe?"

"No, thanks, Tony. Actually, I came by tonight to talk to Brynn about Kelly's surgery tomorrow. I thought you might have some questions," he added when she looked quickly at him.

"As a matter of fact, I do. I'd hoped to have a chance to talk to you before the operation."

"Yes, well...we seemed to have kept missing each other at the hospital this week." He didn't see a reason to add that he'd been very careful to arrange it that way. "Why don't we go to your place and I'll outline the procedure for you and answer your questions."

Michelle reached out to relieve Brynn of Justin. "That's a good idea. You'll be able to talk in peace."

Joe and Brynn were headed for the door when Michelle suddenly called out. "Oh, Brynn, I forgot to tell you...Shane phoned while you and the kids were at the park. He wants you to phone him back sometime this evening. I'm so sorry, I got busy and the call completely slipped my mind."

Brynn nodded. Joe noted in some annoyance that she didn't seem in the least surprised that Shane had called her.

"Thanks, Michelle. I'll phone him later."

It was none of his business, Joe reminded himself as he followed her out. Shane had every right to call Brynn. In fact, he would be an idiot *not* to call her.

But as of tonight, Shane Walker had himself some competition for the lady's attention.

By the time Brynn walked Joe to her door a little over an hour later, she was satisfied that he had answered every question she could think of to ask about Kelly's condition. He had patiently gone over every de-

tail of the surgical procedure—several times, actually—
so that Brynn knew exactly what he was going to do
and why. He'd also been very honest about anything
that could possibly go wrong, though he'd reassured her
that he expected everything to go well.

"You're sure you wouldn't like to go have something
to eat with me?" he asked as he hesitated at the door.

"Thank you, but not tonight. The kids gave me a real
workout today," Brynn admitted with a rueful smile.
"I'm going to spend a quiet evening relaxing and reading, and then I want to be at the hospital early enough
in the morning to see Kelly for a minute before you
take her into surgery."

He nodded. "Okay. Get some rest. But, Brynn..."

Her thoughts still on the operation the next morning,
Brynn gave him only part of her attention as she asked,
"Yes?"

"The next time I invite you to dinner, it won't be as
Kelly's doctor."

It took a moment for the meaning of that firmly spoken statement to sink in. By the time it had, Joe was
gone, the door closed firmly behind him.

Joe was with Kelly when Brynn walked into the hospital room the next morning. At the sight of him, Brynn
felt her cheeks flood with hot color. She looked quickly
away from him, hoping to regain her composure before
she faced him again.

*"The next time I invite you to dinner, it won't be as
Kelly's doctor."*

The words had remained in her head ever since he'd
left her yesterday. She'd spent several hours trying to
convince herself that she'd misunderstood him. That he
hadn't meant what it had sounded like he'd meant. But

then she'd told herself to stop being an idiot. She knew exactly what he'd meant.

Joe was going to ask her out. On a date, not a professional consultation. And she couldn't even claim that she'd had no clue that it was going to happen, eventually. Something had passed between them almost the first time they'd met—and trying to ignore it hadn't made it go away. No matter how foolish she knew it was.

She told herself that Joe would lose interest once he knew the reasons she had no intention of getting involved with him. But she didn't look forward to telling him all the unpleasant details of her past that had brought her to this point. She would rather find a way to convince him that the most they could be was friends, without going into all the reasons why.

But that, she told herself as she glanced at Kelly, was something to deal with later. For now, she had to concentrate on her friend.

"Good morning," she said, looking at Kelly but including them both in the greeting.

"Hi, Brynn!" Kelly's response was a bit louder and more enthusiastic than absolutely necessary. "New dress? It's pretty. Isn't that a pretty dress, Doc?"

Brynn was wearing a royal-blue T-shirt dress she'd owned for three years. Kelly had seen her in it literally dozens of times. Brynn frowned, then glanced at Joe, able now to see him primarily as Kelly's doctor.

"She's been given medication already," he explained with a slight smile.

"I see." Brynn turned back to Kelly. "Are you feeling okay?"

"I feel great!" Kelly grinned. "Doc's going to tighten some screws in my leg—or loosen them—I forget which. I told someone earlier that he was going to screw my leg, but that didn't sound right, somehow.''

"No," Brynn agreed, her voice a bit strained. "That really doesn't sound right. Are you worried about the operation, Kelly?''

"Heck, no.'' Kelly gave Joe another sappy smile. "Doc says he knows what 'he's doing, and I believe him, don't you?''

"Of course.'' Brynn looked again at Joe, knowing her expression was quizzical.

He chuckled. "Some people react more dramatically to meds than others. Kelly's flying.''

Brynn couldn't help smiling. "She gets high on nitrous oxide at the dentist's office. Over-the-counter cold medications put her out for hours. A dentist once told her it's a good thing she's never done drugs, because she reacts much too strongly to them.''

"Have you ever noticed that those little holes in the ceiling start swirling if you stare at them too long?'' Kelly mused aloud, gazing upward in apparent fascination.

Someone cleared his throat. Brynn looked around to find Shane Walker standing in the open doorway.

She clapped a hand to her head. "I was supposed to call you last night. I'm sorry, I completely forgot.''

Joe's parting words had driven the telephone message out of her mind, she realized with an involuntary glance at Joe, who looked strangely pleased about something.

Shane waved a hand. "No problem. You probably had other things on your mind.''

Brynn looked quickly away from Joe. "That's no excuse. I should have called.''

"I was only going to ask if you wanted company in

the waiting room during Kelly's surgery. I happen to have some free time this morning.''

Touched, Brynn smiled. "I'd like that. Thank you.''

Joe, who suddenly appeared more somber, cleared his throat. "We're about ready to get started. If there are no more questions, you two can go on into the waiting room.''

As if in response to his words, a nurse entered. "Dr. D'Alessandro?''

Joe nodded. "We're ready.''

Shane touched Brynn's arm. "I think we're being thrown out.''

She nodded and turned toward the bed. "Kelly, I'll be in the waiting room, okay? I'll see you later.''

"Okay,'' Kelly answered happily. "See you later. T.W.R., Brynn. Hey, *he's* cute,'' she added, catching sight of Shane.

Shane chuckled. "That's what all the women say when they first see me. It's a burden, but one I've learned to bear.''

"Out,'' Joe ordered, pointing to the door. "You can tell more of your lies to Brynn in the waiting room.''

Thanks to Shane's company, the time passed quickly as Brynn waited for word of Kelly's condition. She couldn't help but be amused and diverted by his continuous nonsense. Even when he stopped teasing to talk with her more seriously, she found everything he had to say interesting.

Shane was attractive, funny, smart, charming, and able to converse easily about an amazing variety of subjects. Even though she sensed there was a side to him he would never allow anyone else to see, she liked him a great deal and hoped to become his friend. But she couldn't imagine anything else developing between them. They were as comfortable together as longtime pals, but there wasn't even a spark of chemistry—and Brynn was certain that he felt the same way about her. Which was a great relief, considering the sparks that sizzled when she and Joe were together, an unfortunate development that could eventually drive an awkward wedge between them.

To keep her mind off the operation—and her preoccupation with the doctor—she asked Shane to tell her about the ranch he operated with his father and stepmother. "I understand it's only about thirty miles from here."

He nodded. "That's about right."

"Did you grow up there?"

He shook his head. "No. I lived with my mother and stepfather for most of my childhood. Dad was in the navy and spent a lot of time at sea. He got out when I was twelve and got custody of me, and we lived sort of on the road for a couple of years, doing ranch work while he saved up for a place of his own. When he was reunited with my aunts and uncles a little more than ten years ago, he had a chance to buy the ranch. He married Cassie, bought the ranch, and we've been living happily there ever since—except for the four years he insisted I spend away at college."

"What was your major?"

"Business. Dad hates the paperwork part of the operation. And he thinks computers were invented by Satan himself. So I take care of that part."

"You live with your father and stepmother?"

"No. I have my own house. It's on the ranch property, but a quarter mile or so from Dad and Cassie's place. Dad and I built my house when I finished college.

It's not very big, but it's expandable if I ever find some-one I want to share it with.''

"You say that as if it's a very remote possibility.''

He chuckled. "At this point, that's the way it feels. To be honest, I'm not in any hurry to get married or start procreating. I have a few other things I want to do first.''

"I know just how you feel.'' Brynn tried to speak as lightly as he had. "Marriage and kids aren't in my plans for now, either.''

Now or ever, she could have added. But that was something she saw no reason to get into with Shane.

"Brynn?''

She looked up to find Joe standing beside her, dressed in his scrubs and wearing what she was coming to think of as his "doctor face.'' Funny how she was beginning to separate the two sides of him in her mind—the Joe who was Kelly's doctor and the Joe who could make her pulse race with only a look and a smile.

She rose quickly, wondering how much of her con-versation with Shane he'd overheard, then dismissed that thought for more important considerations. "Is it over?''

"Yes. Kelly's in recovery. Everything went well.''

Even though he'd assured her repeatedly that this op-eration was relatively routine for him and that he hadn't expected complications, Brynn was greatly relieved that it was over. "Thank God.''

"You'll be able to see her in a while. She'll be groggy, and in some pain today, but that's to be ex-pected.''

Brynn turned to Shane. "I know you have things to do today. Don't feel that you have to hang around here with me. Michelle's spending the day with the kids, so

I'm planning to spend most of the day here with Kelly. But thank you so much for coming to keep me company during the operation. That was very thoughtful of you.''

Shane tossed a boyish lock of dark hair off his forehead and grinned, flashing his wicked dimples. ''That's what friends are for, right?''

Friends. It was very nice to know she had made some very good ones in the past couple of weeks. She smiled when Shane leaned over to brush a kiss across her cheek.

''Give me a call if you need anything,'' he said; then, with a nod to Joe, turned and strolled out of the waiting room with that rolling cowboy walk that probably caused feminine hearts to flutter all over Dallas.

Unfortunately, there was only one man who made Brynn's heart misbehave, and he was standing much too close for comfort, wearing a frown she couldn't quite interpret.

''I have another operation scheduled in a half hour. Are there any other questions you need to ask me before I go talk to the other family?''

She shook her head. ''No, I think you've answered all my questions for now. Thank you.''

''I'll call you later.''

''It's really not—''

''I'll call you,'' he interrupted, and he wasn't speaking as Kelly's doctor now.

He turned and walked out of the waiting room before she could think of anything else to say. She noticed that she wasn't the only woman who watched him leave.

Those other women would probably think Brynn an idiot for worrying that Joe was going to ask her out. He was gorgeous, single, successful, amusing. The kind of man most single women her age fantasized about attracting.

But Brynn wasn't like most single women. While she might have her fantasies, she knew that they were best left at that. If she'd ever seen a man who would want a wife and a house full of kids, it was Joe D'Alessandro. And Brynn had nothing to offer him when it came to that.

That was a dream she'd given up when she was thirteen years old, when she'd learned the painful lesson that some dreams simply weren't meant to come true.

Not for her, anyway.

Chapter Eight

The entire Walker family, with the exception of the married sister who lived in Arkansas, gathered at Jared's ranch Saturday for a cookout. Though she hesitated when Michelle and Tony invited her, Brynn was persuaded to join the party when Jason, Carly and Katie shamelessly begged her to go.

The ranch was lovely, consisting of acres of rolling pastureland surrounding a trim, brick-and-siding ranch house and several well-maintained outbuildings. Shane's smaller, white frame bungalow was visible from the main house but far enough away to provide plenty of privacy.

The large, fenced backyard was filled almost to capacity with the family who'd gathered for the occasion. Brynn struggled to remember names and mentally group family units.

Jared, Cassie, Shane and Molly were easy enough to

remember. Kevin and Layla Samples had brought their three teenagers, Dawne, nineteen, Keith, sixteen, and thirteen-year-old Brittany, whom Brynn had already met. Joe and Lauren were there with their ten-year-old son, Casey, and Ryan and Taylor with their seven-year-old twins, Andrew and Aaron. Tony and Michelle's three older children dashed happily into the midst of their young cousins.

Brynn was struck by the physical similarities among the Walker siblings. They all had brown hair—though some were beginning to gray, and the twins, Joe and Ryan, had more gold blended among the brown in theirs. They were all blue-eyed, though again the twins stood out because their eyes were such a light blue compared with the near navy of the others.

As had happened before, Brynn was drawn into the group warmly and without hesitation. She'd had friends in Longview, of course, but she'd never quite been accepted as quickly as she was by this clan. She remembered Joe's comment that the Walker and D'Alessandro families had expanded so quickly that they had grown accustomed to regularly welcoming newcomers. Perhaps that explained why she'd never been made to feel like an outsider when she joined them.

Dozens of lawn chairs had been grouped in shady areas of the lawn to encourage conversation among the adults while the children ripped and played around them. They sipped iced tea and swapped family gossip before beginning the process of feeding everyone.

It turned out that Cassie and Jared occasionally took in foster children at their ranch. Cassie mentioned that when she announced, "We got a call last week about another boy. He's fourteen, and his mother is ill. He's been living with his grandmother, but she's finding it difficult to keep up with him. The social worker thought he might benefit from the structure and honest hard work of a ranch.''

Tony frowned and glanced at Molly, who was leading her younger cousins in a rowdy game of Mother May I. ''You aren't worried that he might be a problem for Molly?''

''We let all the boys know from the beginning that we will tolerate no misbehavior, especially where Molly's concerned,'' Jared said, his expression one that would probably make any teenage boy quake. ''And we've taught her exactly what to do if any boy ever does anything that makes her the least uncomfortable. She doesn't hesitate to talk to us about anything.''

Cassie nodded. ''We've never had any real problems with the few boys we've taken in. Jared's favorite foster home was a ranch, and he follows the example his foster father there set for him.''

Brynn thought again that it was nice to be around people who'd had enough experience with the foster care system that they weren't uncomfortable with her background.

Cassie glanced at her watch. ''We'd better start cooking. I'm getting hungry, and those burgers and dogs aren't going to jump on the grills themselves.''

Apparently, they'd done this enough to have a routine down. Everyone seemed to have a chore to do to get the meal prepared. Everyone except Brynn. She asked Layla what she could do to help.

A twinkle in her eyes, Layla motioned Shane over. ''We really have plenty of help. Why don't you show Brynn around the ranch until the meal is ready, Shane.''

''I'd be delighted,'' Shane replied with a flash of

dimples. He crooked an arm in Brynn's direction. "Shall we?"

Smiling, she slid her hand into the bend of his elbow. "You're sure there's nothing I can do to help?" she asked Layla again.

"Shh," Shane warned loudly. "She's liable to think of something. You make a great excuse to get me out of grilling hot dogs."

"Not exactly gentlemanly, Shane," Layla chided fondly.

"True. But honest," he commented with a laugh.

His obviously adoring aunt shook her head. "Go entertain your guest."

Brynn noted that several of Shane's aunts and uncles looked at them in approval as they headed toward a large barn. She bit her lip.

"Hmm. Seems some of my relatives have decided to try their hand at matchmaking." Shane didn't sound particularly perturbed by the prospect.

"I, er, hope none of them are getting the wrong idea. That you and I are anything more than friends, I mean," she added a bit awkwardly.

He shrugged. "You and I know the truth. I like you very much, Brynn."

"I like you, too," she replied, relieved that his words appeared to have no hidden meaning. He'd already made it clear that he wasn't ready to settle down, and she'd said the same to him.

Now they could concentrate on cementing their budding friendship without worrying about either of them getting the wrong idea.

Joe arrived at the Walker ranch just as the food was being arranged on the tables that had been set out for the occasion.

Tony spotted him first. "Hey, *fratello*. Good timing, as always. You're here just in time to eat."

"Sorry I'm late. Something came up at the hospital."

Layla smiled. "We're just glad you could join us today."

He kissed her cheek. "Thank you, Layla. By the way, you're looking beautiful, as always."

She blushed in pleasure.

The children noticed him then, and Joe was busy for the next few minutes dealing with greetings for "Dr. Joe." He finally had a chance to greet the adults. But he was very aware that someone was missing.

He glanced at Tony. "I, er, thought Brynn was joining you today."

"Brynn's here. She's off somewhere with Shane," Layla said, looking rather smug about it.

Michelle chuckled. "Layla has decided Shane and Brynn make a cute couple."

Layla smiled without embarrassment. "Well, they do. They're the same age, and both of them are unattached. Why shouldn't they be encouraged a little?"

Joe could think of several reasons. None of which he intended to go into at the moment.

He noticed that Tony was giving him an odd look. Joe made an effort to clear his expression. "So, where's the food?" he asked.

Michelle took his arm. "Right this way."

Brynn had been laughing at something nonsensical Shane said when she spotted Joe watching her from among the group gathered around the picnic tables. Her smile faded.

She hadn't known he was going to be here.

Katie was sitting on Joe's lap, a finger in her mouth, her head nestled in his shoulder. She was obviously tired from the ripping and romping she'd been doing with her cousins. Brynn knew it would take only a few minutes of rest before Katie was ready to go full steam again.

Joe looked so utterly natural with a small child in his lap, his hand stroking her back with an absent, but so genuine, affection. He was a man who loved his family, who treasured each one of them, who would make a wonderful father, just as his own father had been.

Maybe if Brynn had had a father like Vinnie—any father, at all—she wouldn't have to turn away when a wonderful man like Joe D'Alessandro looked her way, she thought with an old, sad wistfulness.

Shane put a hand on Brynn's shoulder. "We timed this just right, didn't we? They're just setting out the food. I don't know about you, but I'm starving."

She forced a smile as she looked up at him. "Something tells me you say that a lot."

"Hey, I'm a growing boy," he protested. "I need my vitamins."

Since this "boy" was a well-developed man of nearly six feet, Brynn snorted inelegantly. "Yeah, right."

Brynn wasn't sure how she ended up sitting between Joe and Shane during the meal. Dawne, Keith and Brittany Samples sat across from them. The younger children sat on quilts spread on the grass, while the five married couples took the other two tables that had been set up.

It didn't seem to bother Joe to be the only one at their table over thirty. He talked easily with the teenagers, discussing current music and movies with Brittany, sports and computer games with Keith and the future of medical research with Dawne, who was studying microbiology at UT-Dallas. Shane kept the conversation moving even faster with his teasing and joking, making the girls giggle and Keith snicker.

Brynn didn't contribute much to the conversation, responding only when she was drawn in by the others. She was so acutely aware of Joe sitting at her side, his thigh occasionally brushing hers—by accident?—that she could hardly swallow her food. The fact that Shane sat just as closely at her other side and didn't have at all the same effect on her didn't escape her attention.

She was pathetic, she told herself grimly. No matter how often she told herself this infatuation with Joe D'Alessandro was a foolish and ultimately dangerous fantasy, she couldn't seem to get past it.

After eating, the children, refreshed and re-energized, wanted to ride on horseback. Jared and Shane obligingly saddled three gentle mares and conducted a riding session, taking the smallest tots in the saddle with them, letting the older ones ride alone but with close supervision. Molly, who'd been on horseback since before she could walk and had a wallful of barrel-racing ribbons and trophies to prove her love for it, eagerly gave riding tips to her cousins who weren't quite as experienced at the sport.

"Do you ride, Brynn?" Joe asked, leaning against the corral fence beside her as they watched the children's antics along with the other adults.

"No," she admitted. "I haven't been on a horse since I was a small child and sat on a pony for a photograph."

Overhearing, Ryan Walker clutched his chest in surprise. "Raised in Texas and you don't ride? That's almost sacrilegious, isn't it?"

Riding around the corral with Katie on the saddle in front of him, Shane called out, "I'll take you riding when I'm finished here, Brynn."

"No. I'll take her." Joe looked at Cassie. "Okay if we take Storm and Sunshine?"

Looking a bit speculatively from Brynn to Joe, Cassie nodded. "Of course. They're in their stalls, saddled up. We thought some of the adults might want to ride. Help yourself."

"Oh, but I—"

Ignoring Brynn's protest, Joe took her arm and all but towed her toward the barn. "Trust me," he said. "You'll have fun."

Ten minutes later, Brynn reluctantly allowed herself to be lifted into the saddle on a pretty little golden mare that Joe had told her was Cassie's favorite. Speaking as impersonally as if he were a professional riding instructor and she a paying student, he placed the reins in her hands and gave her a list of basic instructions, assuring her that Sunshine was a well-behaved lady who would be very patient with Brynn's mistakes. He fretted a bit that Brynn had worn loafers with her jeans and mint-green T-shirt—loafers, he muttered, had a nasty way of sliding out of the stirrup—but she assured him that she would be careful.

Once he was confident that she was securely mounted, he turned to the larger, black horse he'd called Storm. Brynn watched as Joe placed one booted foot into the left stirrup and swung his right leg easily over the horse's back. In his denim shirt, jeans and boots, his usually neat hair ruffled by the spring breeze, Joe looked more like a cowboy than a physician, and Brynn couldn't resist telling him so.

He grinned. "Jared and Shane would probably laugh if they heard that. I grew up a Dallas city-kid, remember? I was hardly ever on a horse until ten years ago, when I got to know them. Jared taught me to ride while I was still a medical student and would come home for breaks whenever I got a spare weekend."

"You seem to be a natural at it," she commented, watching as he wheeled Storm toward a path that led them away from the activities going on at the other side of the barn. She clutched her own reins when Sunshine followed at an easy walk.

"Yeah, well, you haven't seen Jared and Shane in action with their horses. I've accused them of communicating telepathically with the animals. Jared works magic with even the highest-strung horse, and Shane has them following him around like adoring puppies. I've seen him rodeo a few times. He and Runaway— his gelding—are a team, both of them seeming to understand the other perfectly."

Balancing carefully, and a bit awkwardly, on the hard saddle, Brynn tried to pay attention to her riding and the conversation at the same time. "Shane rodeos? I didn't know that."

"It's not a full-time thing for him. He's a rancher at heart, but he likes to compete occasionally."

"Isn't it dangerous?"

Joe's mouth kicked into a half smile. "Are you asking me to speak as a native Texan or an orthopedic surgeon? I've seen entirely too many broken bones resulting from the sport, but there's a longtime fascination with it I can't quite deny. Grip with your knees a little more, Brynn. And don't hold the reins so tight—Sunshine isn't going to run off with you.''

Brynn tried to relax her grip. The path they followed turned and dipped into a shallow hollow that cut through a stand of trees. She could still hear the faint drift of voices and laughter from behind her, but the trees blocked her view of the houses and barns. Ahead of her, the path continued down to what appeared to be a small stream. Farther in the distance, through breaks in the trees, she could see more rolling pastures, dotted with the cattle Jared and Shane raised.

Though she knew ranch life was hard work and occasionally high stress, Brynn could see the appeal in the life as she soaked in the late-afternoon sunshine, and breathed in the fresh country air. A cow mooed in the distance, echoed by the higher-pitched bawl of a calf.

She clutched the saddle horn as Sunshine lurched over a rough patch of ground. Joe rode so easily and comfortably on Storm that Brynn was embarrassed by her own awkwardness. ''You know where we're going, I assume?''

''Just down to the stream and back. I think that's far enough for your first ride.''

She looked at the shadows lengthening around them. ''What time is it?'' she asked, having forgotten to put on her watch that morning.

Joe glanced at his left wrist. ''Just after six.''

She tried to keep the conversation going to distract Joe from her decidedly amateur riding. ''It's been a lovely day. The Walkers seem to thoroughly enjoy being together.''

''They do. They know how lucky they are to have found each other. They don't take the time they spend together for granted.''

Brynn thought of how much fun Jason, Carly and Katie seemed to be having. "It's especially nice for the children to have so many cousins to play with."

"Yeah. I always had dozens of cousins as playmates when I was growing up. I'm still close to several of them. I'm glad Tony's kids have cousins on both sides of the family for friends."

Brynn was aware that her involuntary sigh was a wistful one. She hoped Joe hadn't noticed.

She should have known better.

"You're thinking of your own childhood?" he asked, reining Storm close to Sunshine's side.

She nodded. "I used to pretend I had a big family," she admitted a bit sheepishly. "My imaginary friends included grandparents, aunts, uncles and cousins. I knew all their names and even wrote out elaborate descriptions of them in my 'secret' notebooks."

"That sounds so sad."

She avoided his sympathetic eyes. "It was a way of entertaining myself when I was lonely. That was before I knew Kelly, of course."

"You said your parents had no families to take you in?"

"No. I think I mentioned that my parents met in a home for orphaned teenagers. They'd both been in foster care for years. Mama told me my father was her first boyfriend. He died in a car accident when she was three months pregnant. She...never got over that tragedy."

"You said you were thirteen when she died?"

She nodded, choosing not to go into the details of her mother's death. "Even before she died, I spent most of my childhood in foster care. Mama was only seventeen when I was born, and she really wasn't equipped to raise a child on her own."

"But you still saw her often?"

Brynn shrugged. "On and off."

"Did you love her?"

Startled by the question, Brynn bit her lip. No one had ever asked her that before. She didn't know how to answer. Had what she felt for her troubled young mother been love? Or had she only wanted to love her? Had the anger she still sometimes felt when she thought about her childhood destroyed any warmer feelings she might have had for the woman who'd been so sadly ill-equipped to be the kind of parent Brynn had longed for?

"Sorry," Joe murmured when Brynn continued to hesitate. "That's a personal question. I shouldn't have asked."

She risked a glance at him. "It's okay. I just don't know how to answer."

"Then don't." He smiled suddenly and kneed Storm into a somewhat faster pace. "Follow me."

As if she had a choice. Sunshine fell into step just behind Storm, and Brynn wouldn't have known how to guide the horse differently if she'd wanted to. All she could do was cling to the saddle and try to stay balanced as Joe rode Storm directly into the shallow stream and Sunshine followed.

Cool water splashed upward from the horses' hooves. Sunshine sidestepped a few large rocks, making Brynn shift in the saddle. She clutched the saddle horn even more tightly.

"If I fall off this horse…" she warned Joe, her voice higher pitched than usual.

He flashed her a grin. "Yes?"

"I'll expect you to put the broken bones back together."

"It would be my pleasure."

"Now, why doesn't that make me feel better?" She gulped and adjusted her weight quickly when Sunshine stumbled slightly on the uneven stream bottom. "Joe!"

He was laughing now, the insensitive male. "You're doing fine. I think we'll go back to the barn at a full gallop. I know, let's race. Once Storm starts running, Sunshine will, too."

Though he was teasing—or, at least, she sincerely hoped he was—Brynn gave Joe a glare. "Don't even think about it."

He chuckled again, then wheeled Storm. "Lead her into a left turn. That's right, just a gentle pressure on the reins. You really are riding well for your first time, Brynn."

His casual praise pleased her more than it probably should have. To hide her reaction, she concentrated even more intently on her riding.

Back at the barn, Joe instructed Brynn to wait while he dismounted, so he could assist her. He closed Storm into his stall, and the big, black horse was already noisily munching feed when Joe turned to help Brynn.

Standing at Sunshine's left, Joe nodded to Brynn. "Okay. Put your weight on your left foot and swing your right leg over. Hold on to the saddle horn for balance, but don't drop the reins yet."

She carefully followed his instructions. She lowered herself to the ground, then immediately staggered when her knees trembled. Joe's hands closed instantly around her waist. She automatically clutched his forearms for balance.

His voice held a note of sympathetic amusement. "It takes a minute or two to steady your legs after your first couple of rides."

Embarrassed again, she frowned. "We didn't ride that long. I wasn't expecting to be so wobbly."

"You held your muscles tensed the entire time. It gets easier when you learn to relax in the saddle. The more you ride, the better you get at it."

"I don't know that I'll ever ride enough to qualify as a horsewoman, but thank you for the lesson."

"I enjoyed it."

She was suddenly aware that he was still standing very close to her, his hands on her sides, his breath warm on her face. Her own hands were still resting on his forearms, and she could feel the firm bulge of muscle beneath her fingertips.

Her face flooded with a warmth that mirrored the heat pooling inside her. She tried to move away, but Joe held her in place.

"Brynn."

She cleared her throat. "Yes?"

"Why do you always stop smiling when you see me?"

Apparently, this was his day for asking questions she didn't know how to answer. "I don't—"

"Yes, you do," he cut in when she tried to deny his words. "You laugh with Shane, but you stop when you see me. Is it something I've done?"

"Of course not." Flustered, she lowered her lashes.

He caught her chin in his right hand and lifted her face so she was compelled to look at him. His dark eyes bored into hers, seeming to see right into her. "I want you to smile for me, Brynn."

She had rarely felt less like smiling. He was standing so close. His fingers were so warm on her face. His beautifully shaped mouth was only inches from hers.

How could she smile when all she could think about was how it would feel to kiss him?

Maybe he really *could* see straight into her mind. Something flared in his eyes. His fingers tightened at her waist, drawing her an inch closer to him.

"Brynn." His voice had gone husky.

Her fingers clenched reflexively on his forearms. Her own voice was a mere whisper. "Joe, we…"

"Hey, Brynn. How was your ride?"

Knowing her cheeks were scarlet, and praying Shane would attribute her high color to her ride, Brynn whirled away from Joe, who made no attempt to detain her this time.

"It was…very nice," she said, smoothing her damp palms down the legs of her jeans. "Sunshine was very patient with me."

Seeming to notice nothing out of the ordinary, Shane patted Sunshine's neck. "Sunny's a sweetheart, aren't you, baby?"

Sunshine blew air from her nostrils, lifted her head and gave Shane an adoring horsey kiss.

"Is there any lady you *can't* charm, Shane?" Michelle asked in feigned exasperation, strolling through the open barn door.

With patently fake modesty, Shane dragged a booted toe through the dust. "Aw, shucks, ma'am. You're embarrassing me."

Michelle snorted in disbelief. "As if *that* were possible." Turning her back on her nephew, she smiled at Brynn. "Did you enjoy your ride?"

Somewhat more in control now, Brynn deliberately avoided looking at Joe. "Yes, very much."

"Good. Tony and I have to go now. The baby's getting fussy and Tony has a few calls to make this evening. Are you ready to leave now or would you like to stay a little longer and catch another ride back?''

"You can ride with me, Brynn."

Still looking at Michelle, Brynn said, "Thank you, Joe, but I'll go with Tony and Michelle and the children. I'm ready to leave, anyway. I'd like to take a quick shower and visit Kelly a few minutes this evening."

She could sense that he wasn't pleased with her answer, but she didn't give him a chance to try to change her mind. She patted Sunshine, then moved quickly to Michelle's side. "I'm ready."

It took nearly twenty minutes to tell everyone goodbye, thank Cassie and Jared for hosting the party and persuade the D'Alessandro children to get into the minivan. Brynn didn't breathe easily again until they were underway, Carly and Katie competing for her attention as they verbally replayed every minute of their day. She listened patiently to their babbling, responded when given the opportunity and then chatted with Tony and Michelle and Jason when the exhausted girls fell asleep barely halfway into the ride home.

Even as she carried on a coherent conversation and pretended she'd enjoyed every moment of the day, Joe's voice haunted her, his words echoing in her mind:

"Why do you always stop smiling when you see me?"

Chapter Nine

"So then Jared and Shane gave the children horseback rides and Joe and I rode to a stream and back, and by then it was time to come home." Brynn concluded her recitation of the day's events in the same casual, breezy tone she'd used throughout the visit with Kelly, who'd demanded to hear every detail.

"It sounds like so much fun." Kelly's voice was wistful. "I'd have loved to be there, if only to see *you* on horseback."

Brynn smiled ruefully. "I'm not sure it was such an inspiring sight. I felt so awkward and klutzy in comparison with Jared and Shane and Joe. And you should see Molly ride. Ten years old and she's already a champion."

Sitting up in the raised hospital bed, supported by pillows, Kelly studied her friend's face. "You like them, don't you?"

"Yes, of course. They're all very nice."

"Do you find anyone particularly 'nice'?"

Brynn studied her fingernails. "I like them all. You will, too, once you get to know them, as I'm sure you will, since you'll be living in the guest house with me when you're released."

"You didn't answer my question. Tell me about Shane."

Brynn couldn't help smiling when she pictured Shane. She imagined most people who knew him smiled at the thought of him.

"He's very funny. Charming. Sweet. Animals, children and little old ladies adore him. Everyone else genuinely likes him. There's a hint of darkness in his eyes every once in a while—as if he has a few bad memories he doesn't like to dwell on. But he seems to be able to shrug off whatever bothers him and find a way to make himself—and everyone around him—laugh."

"You're fond of him."

"Yes. He's become a friend, and you know how much real friendship means to me."

"Now tell me about Joe."

"Joe Walker? He's the serious one of the twins. Ryan's quite the cutup, but Joe…"

"Brynn." Kelly interrupted patiently. "You're being deliberately obtuse. I was talking about Joe D'Alessandro."

Brynn plucked at a minute speck of lint on her black slacks. "What can I tell you about him? You've known him as long as I have."

"I know him as my doctor. Tell me what he's like away from the hospital."

Brynn bit her lip. "Well, he's, uh…" She trailed off lack of words.

''You've stopped smiling.''

Kelly's murmured comment startled Brynn into a scowl. Kelly couldn't realize, of course, how significant her observation was in light of the similar one Joe had made.

''I was just trying to think of the right words,'' she said defensively.

''You didn't have any trouble finding words to describe Shane.''

''That's different. Shane is easy to describe. Joe is…a bit more of a challenge.''

''Don't you like him?''

''Of course.'' The reply was automatic. But true, nonetheless. ''He loves his family—his parents, his brothers, his nieces and nephews. He even spoke fondly of his cousins. He's a good doctor, as we've seen for ourselves. He's very intelligent and perceptive and considerate of others.''

''Does he make you laugh—the way Shane does?''

He made her burn—the way no one else ever had. But Brynn couldn't say that, not even to Kelly. She was startled enough to have voiced the unwelcome truth to herself.

''He's not like Shane,'' she repeated. ''Do you want me to tell you about the others I met today?''

''No. As you've said, I'll probably meet some of them. I think you've told me what I wanted to know.''

Brynn didn't like her friend's tone. She shot her a suspicious look, which Kelly returned with a bland smile.

''I suppose the children had a wonderful time today.''

Brynn relaxed a bit at the change of subject. ''Yes, they had a ball. Played until they were so tired they drooped. Jason and Casey, Joe and Lauren's eight-year-old son, are best friends. Jason talks about Casey all the time.''

''So what's on your agenda for the upcoming week, Nanny Brynn?''

Brynn counted off the scheduled activities on her fingertips. ''Dance lessons Monday afternoon for the girls, piano lessons Tuesday for all three, soccer practice every afternoon for Jason and Carly. There's an activity session at the children's museum Thursday morning, and Katie has a doctor's appointment Thursday afternoon, so I'll be watching the baby and the other two until Michelle and Katie return. A new Disney movie opens Friday, and the kids want me to take them to that. Michelle wants to spend all day Wednesday with them, so I'll have that day off.''

''Whew. Busy week.''

''Busy children are less likely to misbehave. They're angels until they get bored, and then they start to squabble. I've been keeping them occupied with the art projects and simple science projects we used at the day-care center, when we don't have other activities planned. I've got a lot more of those to fall back on, fortunately.''

''You sound as though you're enjoying your new job.''

''Well, I've only been at it for a week, but I have enjoyed it so far. It's nice having just a few children to concentrate on instead of the larger groups I was responsible for at the day-care center. It lets me get to know them better.''

Kelly suddenly looked a bit worried. ''Almost like having a family of your own?''

Brynn's smile died. ''No. I'm well aware that I'm only the nanny. I won't lose my professional objectivity or overstep the boundaries of my position in the household. I don't even intend to make a habit of attending family gatherings like the one today.''

Kelly sighed. ''I'm certainly not telling you how to do your job, Brynn. I just want you to be careful. I would hate to see you get hurt if something goes wrong and you have to find another job and another place to live.''

''You don't have to worry about that. As fond as I am of the children, I know it's just a job. And, however it turns out, I'll land on my feet. I always do, remember?''

''Right. And so do I. When my feet aren't strapped down, that is.'' Kelly glared fiercely at her broken legs.

''T.W.R., Kel.'' It was the motto they'd adopted for themselves when they were teenagers. T.W.R. Together We Rule.

Kelly smiled sweetly at her honorary older sister. ''T.W.R., Brynn. Whatever happens, we'll get through it. Together.''

With another silent prayer of gratitude that she hadn't lost Kelly in that accident, Brynn returned the smile.

As Brynn had predicted, the next few days were busy, but pleasant. She enjoyed the time she spent with the children, and had little trouble from them. The few times they did quarrel or misbehave, she had only to speak firmly to them and they subsided, though stubborn Carly usually required a second warning. On the whole, Brynn found her position just challenging enough to keep it from being boring.

She neither saw nor heard from Joe during the first part of the week. After their brief interlude in Jared's barn, she'd half expected him to call her. She told herself she was relieved that he didn't. She had to tell herself several times before she sounded convincing.

When her phone rang Tuesday evening, just after she'd returned from her daily visit to the hospital, her heart tripped. It was probably Shane, she thought, or maybe Michelle with a change of plans for the next day. It probably wasn't Joe. But her palms were damp when she reached for the receiver.

"Hello?"

"Brynn. How are you?"

"Vinnie?" She recognized the voice with pleasant surprise. "I'm fine, thank you. And you?"

"Yes, fine. I called about tomorrow. I understand you're going car shopping."

She wondered for a moment how he knew, then realized that the D'Alessandro family were in frequent contact. Tony must have mentioned Brynn's plans to his father.

"Yes. I have to turn the rental car in tomorrow, and I'll need something else to drive. The check for my car arrived from the insurance company today. It isn't enough to buy a new car, but I'll be able to make a down payment on a good used car."

"Will you let me accompany you? I've had some experience with car salesmen. They know better than to try to outsmart me. They see a pretty young woman alone, and they think they can charge more."

"Thank you, Vinnie, but there's no need for you to go to that trouble. I'm sure I can handle the car salesmen." After all, she reminded herself, she'd bought her last car without assistance. It hadn't exactly been a luxury vehicle, but she'd gotten a fair deal for it. Sort of.

"You'd be doing me a favor to let me go with you. I get restless here by myself while Carla's in court. I like to feel useful. But if you'd rather go alone, I'll understand.''

Brynn couldn't help smiling a little at his tone. He made it sound as if he'd be crushed if she turned him down. And, even though she suspected he was exaggerating a bit, and even though she'd told herself she was going to keep more distance between herself and her employers' families, she found herself unable to refuse Vinnie's kindhearted offer.

''I would love to have your company, Vinnie. Thank you.''

''That's fine, then.'' He sounded quite pleased with himself. ''What time shall we begin?''

''Michelle's going to spend all day tomorrow with the children. I had planned to start shopping at around ten tomorrow morning. Is that too early?''

''Not at all. I'll see you then.''

Brynn was still smiling when she hung up.

Vinnie D'Alessandro was impossible to resist, she mused as she walked into her bedroom. Her smile faded as Joe's image popped vividly into her mind, along with the old saying, ''Like father, like son.''

Both father *and* son were on her front step when Brynn opened her door the next morning. The broad smile she'd worn to welcome Vinnie froze when she saw Joe. She couldn't seem to hold on to it, even though she knew he would notice that she'd once again stopped smiling at the sight of him.

He looked as gorgeous as always in a designer sport shirt and khakis, his wavy dark hair brushed casually back from his face. Brynn pushed her hands self-consciously into the pockets of the navy slacks she'd worn with a short-sleeved plaid shirt.

"Joe. I...didn't expect to see you. I thought you'd be working today."

He shrugged. His easy smile did not reach his dark eyes. "I had early rounds at the hospital, but I take most Wednesdays off. I called Dad this morning to see if he wanted to play golf and he told me you were going car shopping. I invited myself along. I hope you don't mind."

"Of course not," she lied. "But, really, you two should go enjoy your golf game. It's such a beautiful day it's a shame to waste it looking at cars. I'm quite capable of handling this purchase myself."

"I have no doubt of that," Joe said, and looked as though he meant it. "But, as it happens, Dad and I like car shopping almost as much as golf."

Vinnie nodded. "We like poking our heads under hoods and kicking tires and hassling salesmen. Sometimes we do it just for fun."

Brynn could tell she might as well resign herself to Joe's presence. Neither he nor Vinnie showed any inclination to opt out of the excursion.

Another day spent with Joe. Just the thought of it made her grit her teeth in despair. How was she ever going to get over this foolish infatuation with him if she kept spending time with him like this?

She told herself she'd simply have to buy the first suitable, affordable vehicle she found, just to keep the outing as brief and impersonal as possible.

She should have known that wasn't going to be an option.

"What's wrong with *this* one?" she asked nearly three hours later as she faced Joe's and Vinnie's identical expressions of disapproval.

Joe almost curled his lip as he glared at the plain,

boxy little car she'd indicated. ''Besides being incredibly boring? It's a piece of…junk.''

Vinnie nodded somberly. ''I have to agree. The tires are almost bald, there's a dent in the right rear fender and I think I see a few spots of rust forming. You don't want this one, *carina*.''

''This is at least the tenth car you guys have vetoed today. How am I going to find anything if neither of you likes any of the cars in my price range?''

''I'm sure we'll find you a decent car,'' Joe assured her. ''But it has to be better than this one, or you'll regret it. It's no bargain if you're setting yourself up for a lot of expensive repair bills.''

Brynn sighed, unable to argue with that logic. ''We'll keep looking.''

''Right.'' Joe glanced at his watch. ''It's almost one. I'm starving. Why don't we take a lunch break?''

''I could eat.'' Vinnie rubbed his hands together. ''What shall we have?''

It looked as though she'd be lunching with them. She could hardly refuse, since they were spending the day helping her—whether she required their assistance or not. It would be churlish to make them go hungry.

Joe said he was in the mood for Chinese. Vinnie gave the suggestion a few moments of serious thought, then nodded as if he'd reached a momentous decision. ''Chinese sounds good. Brynn, is there something you'd rather have?''

Feeling almost fatalistic now, Brynn forced a smile. ''I like Chinese.''

The D'Alessandro men smiled at her in approval, looking so identically endearing that her heart ached. God help her, she was falling for both of them, though in very different ways. Vinnie was the father she'd always dreamed of having. And Joe was a dream in himself.

It seemed inevitable now that her heart was going to be broken eventually. But she'd survived broken hearts and shattered dreams before. She could only hope the defenses she'd spent so many years developing would protect her this time.

Brynn allowed herself to enjoy her lunch. It would have been almost impossible not to, since Vinnie and Joe seemed to go out of their way to entertain her. Maybe they were trying to make up to her because their high standards had kept her from finding a car so far. They succeeded.

The food was delicious, and the service at the small, tastefully decorated Chinese restaurant was impeccable. It turned out that Joe had operated on the owner's mother—a standard hip replacement, he explained—and now he was a valued customer of the establishment. Watching the owner's two pretty young daughters flirt gaily with Joe as they waited the table, Brynn wondered if there was *anyone* who was immune to him.

Vinnie excused himself after lunch to make a couple of calls, promising he'd be back quickly. Brynn and Joe were left alone at the table, steaming cups of hot tea in front of them.

Brynn held her handleless cup in both hands and tried frantically to think of something innocuous to say to fill the silence.

Joe beat her to it. "You did it again today."

She eyed him warily. "Did what?"

"You stopped smiling when you saw me. You opened your door with a big smile for Dad, but it vanished when you saw me."

"I was surprised to see you. I wasn't expecting you."

"Was it such an unpleasant surprise?"

"Of course not."

"Do you dislike me, Brynn?"

"No," she answered, shaking her head fervently.

"Do I intimidate you?"

She hesitated before she answered that one. Intimidate her? He scared her spitless. "I..."

"Some people are intimidated because I'm a doctor. I don't know why, exactly, but they are. Is that it?"

That was certainly part of it. When she was with Joe, Brynn was painfully aware of their different social and educational standings. He could have bought any car he wanted today, while Brynn had to be painfully conscious of price and payments. She was the nanny for his nieces and nephews. He was the son of a judge, accustomed to dating beautiful doctors, like the woman they'd met when they'd dined together the night she'd moved into Michelle's guest house.

When she remained silent for lack of words, Joe sighed and shook his head. "I want to see you smile for me, Brynn. A real smile, not the polite ones you force when you look at me."

"I'll try," she promised. "Will that satisfy you?"

"Not by a long shot," he answered a bit gruffly. "But it would be a good start."

Before she could think of anything to say in response, Vinnie returned, looking quite satisfied with his calls.

"I've got a lead on a car for you," he told Brynn, unaware of her relief that he'd interrupted the unsettling conversation with Joe. "I remembered an old buddy from my police days who started selling used cars when he retired. He said it kept him from getting bored. He told me to bring you by and he'll set you up with something nice and affordable.''

Brynn nodded. "All right. I'd be happy to talk to him.''

"Not just yet.'' Joe reached for the little basket that had been placed in the center of their table. He lifted out something wrapped in crinkly cellophane and handed it to Brynn, his fingers lingering on hers for a bit longer than necessary.

Her pulse skipping from the contact, Brynn stared blankly at what she held. A fortune cookie. It took her a moment to remember how to open it.

Joe didn't just intimidate her. He devastated her.

Vinnie cracked his cookie open while Brynn hesitated. "'Your patience will be rewarded,'" he read aloud.

He chuckled. "Now aren't you glad we didn't buy the first car you saw, Brynn?''

Joe's cookie broke neatly in his hands. "'Success awaits you in the coming year.' Well, that sounds promising. What does yours say, Brynn?''

Brynn's fingers were slightly unsteady when she broke her cookie and extracted the thin slip of paper. She stopped breathing when she read the printed message: *Love finds even the hidden heart.*

"Well?'' Vinnie prodded cheerfully when Brynn continued to stare at the words. "What's it say, *carina?*''

She crushed the paper in her hand. "It says I'm going on a long journey. I hope this one doesn't end as disastrously as the last journey I made almost did.''

She could tell from the way Joe looked at her that he was suspicious about the fortune she'd claimed. She kept her expression blandly innocent as she pushed her chair back from the table and stood, tossing the crumpled fortune onto her empty plate, which hadn't yet been cleared away. "Shall we go see if your friend has a car that will satisfy you two?"

Joe glanced at Brynn's plate, and she knew the fortune that had disconcerted her was on his mind. But he fell quickly back into his former enthusiasm for the hunt for the ideal car.

Brynn wished she could put the message out of her mind as easily. No matter how many times she told herself that cookie fortunes were nothing more than obscure homilies penned by fortune-cookie-factory employees, that they had no particular meaning and only gullible fools took them seriously, she couldn't quite shake the eerie feeling that had gripped her when she'd read those words.

Love finds even the hidden heart.

Two hours later, Brynn was the owner of a little blue sedan. Joe and Vinnie had looked over every inch of it and concluded that it was in excellent condition and was well worth the price Vinnie's old friend quoted them. Vinnie persuaded the man to expedite the paperwork so that Brynn could take possession of the car immediately; he even offered to co-sign the loan, if necessary.

Joe had met his father at Brynn's earlier, and they'd left his two-seater parked in front of her house while they'd shopped in Vinnie's bigger car. "There's no need for you to drive me all the way back to Tony's house, Dad," he said when the transaction was completed. "Brynn can give me a lift in her new car, can't you, Brynn?"

There was only one answer she could give. "Of course."

Vinnie patted the hood of Brynn's car. "You're sure you like it, Brynn?"

"I love it. It's an even nicer car than I expected to find today." On impulse, she rose to kiss his cheek. "Thank you, Vinnie."

"You're very welcome, my dear. I hope you enjoy it."

"I know I will."

"I'll be heading home, then. Carla will be there soon."

"Drive carefully, Dad."

Vinnie waved as he slid behind his steering wheel.

Joe turned to Brynn. "Ready to try her out?"

Brynn opened the driver's door. "Ready."

She would concentrate on her driving, not on her passenger, she vowed.

Ten minutes into the drive, Joe spoke for the first time since they'd left the sales lot. "How do you like it so far?"

"The car? I like it."

Joe looked around the tidy interior in satisfaction. "I think you got a good deal."

"Thanks to you and your father."

He shrugged. "Glad we could help."

Brynn shook her head and couldn't resist saying, "You people are unbelievable."

"What do you mean?"

"Ever since Kelly and I were in that accident, you've all treated us like dear friends. Your parents took me into their house, Tony and Michelle have entrusted me with their children, your dad even offered to co-sign a loan for me, for Pete's sake. It's unreal."

"You had nowhere else to go the night of the accident, you provided references for Tony and Michelle—

and then insisted they verify them—and Dad's a retired ex-cop-turned-P.I. He wouldn't offer to co-sign for you without being reasonably certain you're a good risk. But you wouldn't let him sign, anyway.''

''Fortunately, it wasn't necessary, with the insurance money for a down payment. Still, it's a wonder someone in your family hasn't been victimized by con artists.''

''Who says we haven't?''

Something in Joe's voice made Brynn glance away from the road ahead long enough to study his grim expression. ''I'm sorry. Did I hit a nerve?''

''Not directly. But Michelle's had her share of problems with fortune hunters and an embezzling attorney she had considered a family friend. Trust me, we aren't naïve. It's because we've had experience with crooks and cons that we recognize honesty when we see it.''

''I hate to think of anyone hurting Michelle,'' Brynn said with a frown. ''She's such a nice person. And a wonderful mother. Even with all her business responsibilities, she spends as much time with her children as she can. There are times when I feel almost superfluous. But she says it eases her mind to have someone extra keeping an eye on the children. I suppose it's because of her money that she's so security conscious with the kids.''

''That's exactly the reason. Michelle was kidnapped when she was eight years old, held for three days in a closet until my dad, who'd been hired by her father, found her and brought her home.''

Brynn's hands jerked on the steering wheel, causing the compact car to swerve a bit. She corrected quickly, but she heard the strain in her own voice when she asked, ''Michelle was *kidnapped?*''

"Yes. By a family employee. A man they'd trusted."

"Oh, God." Brynn shuddered, unable to keep herself from picturing a terrified eight-year-old locked in a closet for three long days. "Did he…hurt her?"

"Not physically. There were emotional scars, of course, but she's managed to put it behind her. I told you about it to explain her focus on the children's se- curity—and maybe to remind you of how vulnerable her children are to people who know about the Trent money."

Still shaken, Brynn asked, "Have they ever consid- ered hiring bodyguards?"

"They discussed it briefly when Jason was born, and they decided there was no reason at the time. They want the children to live normal, carefree lives. Having a nanny to watch them while Michelle is busy is as far as they're willing to go."

"I'll never let them out of my sight while I'm re- sponsible for them," she vowed fervently. "I wouldn't have, anyway, but from now on I'll keep all possibilities in my mind."

"There's no need to obsess about it. There's never been a threat against Tony and Michelle's children. It's just something to be aware of."

The large gates to the estate took on new significance when Brynn turned through them. The gates generally remained open during the day but were closed at night. There were other security measures, as well, but none was overly obvious or intrusive.

Brynn had to admire Michelle's determination to make sure her children didn't feel as though they lived in a gilded cage. Given Michelle's background, Brynn wouldn't have blamed her if she'd wanted to keep her children in her direct view every minute of every day.

She turned onto the short driveway leading to the guest house, noting as she passed that Michelle's mini-van and Tony's sport utility vehicle were both gone. It wasn't quite 5 p.m. Tony was probably still at work, and Michelle and the children had made several plans for the day.

She was suddenly vividly aware that she and Joe were alone on the estate, except for the D'Alessandros' housekeeper, who would be leaving at five.

She parked the car and turned off the engine. "Would you like to come in for a drink or something before you go?" she felt compelled to ask. After all he'd done, it seemed rude to just send him on his way without making a hospitable gesture.

"Do you have any cola?"

"Only diet cola."

"That'll do. I'm having a caffeine craving."

Brynn nodded and tried to inject a breezy note in her voice when she said, "Well, come on in, then. We can't have you going into a caffeine fit right here in your brother's backyard."

It was the way she would have spoken to Shane. Casual. Friendly. Teasing. At least, that was the effect she was trying for—even if she simply couldn't imagine ever being as comfortable with Joe as she was with Shane.

Joe responded to her light tone. "It's not a pretty sight," he agreed, opening his door.

Brynn couldn't resist patting the hood of her new car as she walked past. Just three years of payments lay between her and full ownership.

There was amusement in Joe's eyes as he watched

her—and something else that made her walk faster toward her front door. Resisting an ignoble impulse to close that door between them, she held it open for him, instead.

Chapter Ten

"Have a seat," Brynn said, after closing her front door and tossing her purse onto a table. "I'll pour the sodas."

Joe settled onto the couch, stretching one arm across the back, seemingly perfectly at home. He looked as though he planned to stay awhile.

Didn't the guy have anything better to do today?

She moved into the kitchen, where she quickly assembled a tray holding two glasses of iced soda and a plate of the oatmeal-raisin cookies she kept on hand for the children. Intending to sit in one of the two living-room chairs, she set the tray on the coffee table in front of Joe, then straightened. "Help yourself."

He reached out and caught her wrist, giving a gentle tug that had her tumbling down to the couch beside him. "I was hoping you would say that," he said, and his smile had turned wicked.

She gave him a repressive look, though her pulse had begun to race. "I meant help yourself to the soda and cookies."

Joe stroked a fingertip along the line of her cheek— very lightly, making her have to suppress a revealing shiver of reaction. "I'd rather hoped you meant something else entirely."

What had just happened? One moment he'd acted like an old pal, and now he was blatantly flirting. Brynn couldn't switch gears that quickly. He'd caught her completely off-guard.

Had that been his intention?

"Joe, I..."

"Do you know how long I've wanted to kiss you?" He smiled as he spoke, and his tone was conversational, but his eyes were very serious.

Her breath caught in her throat. She tried to speak around it. "We've only known each other a few weeks."

"That doesn't matter. This is something that's been building for a while."

"But..."

"Brynn." He covered her mouth with his fingers and gazed into her eyes. "All you have to say is that you don't want me to kiss you, and I'll back off."

She opened her mouth beneath his fingers to do just that. But the lie wouldn't come out. The truth was, she *wanted* Joe's kiss...almost as much as she feared the consequences. "I..."

When her voice faded, his smile deepened. "I'm going to take that as an answer. Punch me if I've misinterpreted."

He replaced his hand with his mouth before Brynn

could launch into an explanation of why this was such a bad idea.

But it didn't feel like a bad idea, she couldn't help thinking as his lips settled warmly over hers. It felt...incredible.

Her hands lifted reflexively to his shoulders. Her mouth softened instinctively beneath his. Her eyelids drifted downward, feeling suddenly heavy. He kissed, she thought dazedly, as spectacularly as she had fantasized he would.

And, just as she'd feared, she knew nothing would be quite the same for her once the kiss ended.

Joe seemed in no hurry to bring the embrace to a conclusion. His right hand resting lightly against her cheek, he lifted his mouth only enough to change to a new angle, and then he kissed her again.

Brynn's hand lifted almost of its own will, her fingers sliding into the hair at the back of his head. His hair was thick, crisp, and curled lightly around her fingertips. Her other hand still rested on his shoulder. He was solid and strong beneath her palm.

He made her ache in a way no mere kiss had made her ache before.

She almost sighed in protest when he finally, slowly, drew away, leaving her mouth damp, tender and hungry for more.

She hadn't realized she'd begun to tremble until she lowered her hands to rest them in her lap. She could think of nothing to say. Joe's kiss had emptied her mind of rational thought.

"We need to talk." His voice had a hoarse edge to it, proving that he'd been affected by the kiss, as well.

She bit her lip and ducked her head, hiding her face behind her chin-length bob of hair. She didn't want him to see the panic she suspected was mirrored in her eyes, the confusion and dismay she knew were there.

He caught her chin in his hand, lifting her face. "Brynn, I..."

The shrill beeping that interrupted his words made her jump and widen her eyes. It took her a moment to identify the sound.

Joe muttered something she couldn't understand and reached for his belt. The sound stopped. He sighed when he looked at his pager. "I have to leave. I'm sorry, this is lousy timing, but it's very much a part of my job. I never know when I'll be called to work. That's something you should probably know about me before we take this much further."

This? What "this" was he talking about? There was no "this" between them, and if either of them had any sense, there wouldn't be.

She started to tell him just that—a bit more coherently, she hoped—but Joe was already getting up and moving toward the door. He looked regretfully at the cola and cookies as he passed them, and even more regretfully at Brynn when he turned to her at the doorway. "I'll call you," he said.

Still sitting on the couch, she laced her fingers in her lap, not quite trusting her legs to be steady if she rose to see him off. "I think..."

"I'll call you," he repeated firmly, and let himself out, closing the door behind him.

Brynn fell limply against the back of the couch, covering her still-tingling mouth with her hands.

Kissing Joe D'Alessandro had been a grave mistake. Doing so again would be inviting heartbreak.

She sighed and lifted her head. She had things to do. And she needed to keep busy or she would drive herself crazy reliving Joe's kiss. Something caught her eye as she rose from the couch. She glanced down at the slip of crumpled white paper on the cushion next to her.

Thinking it looked a bit like a fortune from a Chinese cookie, like the one she'd left on the table at the restaurant, she picked it up and unfolded it with unsteady hands.

Love finds even the hidden heart.

This man was going to drive her certifiably crazy.

Joe D'Alessandro, Brynn decided during the next few days, was a very conniving man. He must have suspected she would have turned him down if he came out and asked her for a date. So, he didn't ask. He just showed up.

He was there for dinner with his brother and sister-in-law Thursday evening. Before knowing that Joe would be there, Brynn had accepted Michelle's invitation to dine with them. By the time it was mentioned that Joe would be joining them, it was too late to politely change her answer, of course.

Joe sat right beside her at the dinner table. It was suspiciously odd how often his thigh just "happened" to brush against hers during the meal. By the time she'd managed to choke down her dinner, she didn't know whether she wanted more to strangle him or drag him outside and attack him in the bushes.

He insisted on walking her home afterward, as if she lived blocks away instead of a few yards. Brynn was aware that Tony and Michelle watched them speculatively as she and Joe left.

"I always thought doctors were very busy people with almost no free time," she commented as they stepped out into the warm summer evening.

Joe patted the pager clipped to his belt. "Electronics have freed us somewhat. As long as I'm reachable, I've got time for myself after normal working hours."

"I see. Um, I visited Kelly this afternoon. She said you told her she can probably be released in a couple of weeks."

"Yes. She's responding very well, and working hard at her therapy. She should be back on her feet by early fall, though she'll need to support that leg with crutches at first."

"She's still in some pain. She doesn't complain, but I can tell."

He nodded. "I've started cutting back on the pain medication. It's time."

"She'll have medication if she needs it?" Brynn didn't like the idea of Kelly suffering.

"Of course. Kelly will have what she needs and she knows it. She and I have talked about this at length, and she's the one who said she was ready to cut back. None of us want her to become overly dependent on the meds."

"No, of course not."

Joe turned to Brynn at her door. "Kelly's lucky to have such a loyal, caring friend. I envy her."

Brynn was startled by his words. "But you have...everything. A huge, close family. A fabulous career. And you must have dozens of friends."

"All that is true, and I'm not taking any of it for granted. But I'm still going home alone tonight," he remarked gently.

That silenced her, since there was nothing to say in response.

She reached quickly for her door. "Thanks for walking me home, Joe."

His hand covered hers on the doorknob. "Will you ask me in for a little while?"

Just looking at their joined hands, feeling the warmth of his skin next to hers, caused a dull ache in her chest. She didn't look at him when she spoke, her voice strained. "I'm really tired tonight, Joe. It's been a long day."

There was a taut pause, and then Joe sighed in resignation. "Patience," he said, "is not something I'm known for. But for you, I'll work on it."

"Joe, I..."

Once again, he refused to allow her to say anything that would negate any chance of something developing between them. "I'll be seeing you."

He squeezed her hand lightly, then drew away. He was gone before Brynn could find the words to discourage his interest in her—not that she had any idea what she would have said.

Whether by coincidence or design on Joe's part, Brynn happened to be visiting Kelly when Joe stopped in Friday afternoon.

He greeted his patient first, his tone friendly and lightly teasing, his smile warm. And then he turned that smile toward Brynn, and the sudden heat in his eyes nearly melted her kneecaps. It was a very good thing she was sitting down, she thought weakly, hoping she didn't look as dazed as she felt at that moment.

"Hi, Brynn. How's it going?"

"Fine, thanks. Do you need me to leave while you examine Kelly?"

He shook his head as he glanced through Kelly's chart. "I'm just checking in. Therapy go okay today, Kelly?"

"The usual routine. I was brutally tortured, put through incredible pain and agony, folded, spindled and mutilated."

Joe laughed. "Glad it wasn't too bad."

"Hey, Dr. Joe?"

"Yes?"

"When I get my legs back in working condition, I'm going to chase you down and break both of yours."

He didn't look noticeably fazed by the threat. "Well, that just gives you a reason to work harder, doesn't it? It always helps to have a goal."

Kelly sighed gustily. "You see what I have to put up with here, Brynn?"

Brynn nodded gravely. "You surely deserve a medal."

"I heard you had a couple of cowboys in here earlier," Joe said, closing the chart and pulling up the extra chair.

Kelly dimpled and nodded. "I was just telling Brynn about it. Jared and Shane Walker came into town to pick up some supplies for their ranch and they stopped in to visit me. They invited me to come see the ranch and have a riding lesson as soon as I'm able."

"Shane knows how lonely a hospital room can be. He was hospitalized briefly after a car accident when he was a teenager. He wasn't hospitalized nearly as long as you, Kelly, since he wasn't as badly injured, but I can tell you he hated every minute of it. He shudders every time he mentions it."

"I can't imagine Shane being immobilized for long," Brynn commented, smiling a little as she thought of Shane's barely contained energy. "He must have been bouncing off the walls of his hospital room."

"It happened shortly before I met him, so I wasn't

there to see it, but you're probably right," Joe agreed. "Shane's always been a hyper kid."

"Kid?" Kelly giggled. "Shane's hardly a kid. He's three years older than I am—the same age as Brynn."

A fleeting frown crossed Joe's face. "It was a figure of speech. Remember, I've known Shane since he was fourteen and I was in medical school."

"How old are you, Doc?"

Brynn bit her lip, thinking ruefully that Kelly had never been shy about asking personal questions.

"I'm thirty-five. Does that seem ancient to you?"

"Not at all," Kelly assured him with a glance toward Brynn. "Actually, it seems just right."

Brynn narrowed her eyes and sent Kelly a stern mental message. *Be very careful, Kelly.*

But Kelly was wearing the mischievous look that meant someone was going to be embarrassed—usually Brynn.

"So how have you gotten to this ripe, old age without getting married?" she asked Joe with exaggerated innocence.

I'm going to strangle her.

Unaware of Brynn's fierce thought, Joe grinned. "Now you sound like my family. Especially my father."

Kelly wasn't letting him get away without an answer. "So...?"

He shrugged good-naturedly. "I've been in school most of my life. I'm just getting really started in my practice."

"Any serious prospects in the picture?"

Joe lifted an eyebrow. "Why, Miss Morrison, are you flirting with me?"

She batted her eyelashes. "I have to do *something* to entertain myself while I'm in here."

"You could always take up knitting," Brynn suggested dryly.

Joe smiled. "That seems much too tame for her."

"True. She'd probably enjoy kickboxing, but she's not exactly in shape for that at the moment."

Kelly cleared her throat. Loudly. "I *am* still in the room."

Joe chuckled and pushed himself out of his chair. "I've got to be running along. Next time I visit, you can ask me my shoe size and bank balance."

"Oh, I'm sure I can think of more interesting questions to ask you," Kelly murmured.

"Make a list. That will give you something to keep you busy until I see you again."

Joe turned to Brynn, his eyes suddenly gleaming with a slightly wicked smile. "It's always a pleasure to see you, Ms. Larkin."

She couldn't help smiling a little as she responded in the same formal tone. "Thank you, Dr. D'Alessandro."

"I'll see you again soon."

He was whistling beneath his breath when he left.

Brynn stared at the empty doorway until she realized that several long moments had passed in silence. She turned quickly toward the bed, her cheeks warming.

Kelly was looking at her with a glint of speculation. "That," she murmured, "sounded a lot like a promise."

Or a threat, Brynn couldn't help adding silently.

"So when are you going to ask the girl out?"

Lifting an eyebrow in response to his father's impatient tone, Joe looked away from the baseball game playing on the TV. "You're talking to me?"

Vinnie rolled his eyes. "No, I'm talking to your brother."

Lounging on his parents' den couch, his gaze focused on the television screen, Tony sipped his beer and spoke without looking away from the game. "If you're talking to me, then the 'girl' had better be my wife. Michelle would kill me if I asked anyone else out."

"And so she should," Vinnie said sternly. "Only a *bastardo* breaks the vows he makes before God and his wife."

It was talk like that that had kept Joe single for so long. Vinnie and Carla believed absolutely in the sanctity and irrevocability of marriage, and they'd passed their beliefs to their sons. Tony claimed he'd taken one look at Michelle and had known he'd never look twice at another woman.

Joe had been waiting a long time to feel that way about someone.

Vinnie turned his attention back to his youngest son. "Well? I'm waiting for an answer. When are you going to ask her out?"

"By 'her' you mean…?"

"Brynn, of course." Vinnie sounded thoroughly disgusted with Joe's obtuseness. "Who else?"

"*If* I decide to ask a woman out, it will be a woman and a time of my own choosing." Joe turned his attention pointedly back to the game.

Vinnie responded to the hint the way he always did— he ignored it. "She's a nice girl. Pretty, too. And we all know you're interested. Tony said—"

Tony coughed loudly. "Er, Dad…"

Joe glared at his brother and then at his father. "I thought we were going to watch the game."

"The game is boring. I'm more interested in hearing why my son who is smart enough to be a doctor is too dense to know when he meets a woman who is obviously perfect for him."

"That may be obvious to *you,* Dad—and okay, maybe the thought has crossed my mind—but it's certainly not obvious to Brynn. She's given me no reason to believe she wants me to ask her out."

"Michelle thinks she's interested," Tony murmured, looking ready to duck, if necessary.

"Is everyone in the family speculating about my social life?" Joe demanded in exasperation.

"Of course. That's what we D'Alessandros do."

"Well, stop it."

"You bring the girl to Paul and Teresa's for the Fourth of July," Vinnie ordered. "She'll see what a fine family you have, and she'll understand what a fine catch you are."

"You make me sound like a nice fish," Joe muttered. Tony laughed.

"Bring her for the Fourth of July," Vinnie repeated, unperturbed.

"I'm not sure Brynn is entirely comfortable in large family situations. She seems to enjoy being with people, but she always seems more relaxed in small groups."

"The outsider syndrome," Tony murmured.

Joe frowned. "What?"

Tony shrugged. "It's what Jared calls it. He and Joe and Ryan have talked about the adjustments they've had to make since being reunited with their family. Growing up in foster homes, they tended to feel out of place among other families. As if they didn't really belong.

It was something they all had to overcome, even when they first started getting together with their own brothers and sisters and in-laws. Brynn probably feels that outsider syndrome when she's surrounded by D'Alessandros and Walkers. Lacking a family of her own, she's had little experience with the dynamics of large family gatherings.''

"That was very insightful, Antonio."

Tony smiled in response to his father's admiring comment. "I can't take credit for any of it. I was just quoting my in-laws."

Vinnie thought about Tony's comments for a bit longer, then nodded. "I'm sure Brynn has her share of baggage from her foster care experiences, but she seems to have turned out just fine. We wouldn't have her taking care of our little ones otherwise. The children tell me they are already devoted to her. She'll make a good mother to her own children.''

Joe choked on a sip of his beer. He set the can down quickly. "Okay, that's enough. You're talking about Brynn as if she were a broodmare you've been looking over."

Vinnie's brows drew downward. "I've simply pointed out that she's a nice girl—smart, pretty, good with children. We all like her, and we can tell that you do, too. So what's so bad about urging you to do something about it?"

"Just back off, Dad. When it comes to Brynn, I'll make my own decisions."

Apparently deciding he'd pushed as far as he could for now, Vinnie subsided into mutters and returned his attention to the TV. But Joe knew the subject was far from forgotten—by any of them.

* * *

His father's encouragement still echoing in his mind, Joe approached Brynn's door Sunday afternoon. He carried a package in one hand, his excuse for popping in this time. He knew he should have called first, but he'd decided to simply show up unannounced.

Keeping Brynn guessing about him was part of Joe's strategy.

Sometimes, however, his scheming backfired. Joe wasn't at all pleased when Shane Walker answered Brynn's door in response to Joe's knock.

Dressed in a black T-shirt and jeans, Shane looked strong and work toughened, quite different from the skinny fourteen-year-old boy Joe had first met.

"You're here again?" Joe asked, studying Shane's tanned, smug face with narrowed eyes.

Apparently, Shane found something amusing in Joe's tone—but then, Shane generally found something to amuse him in just about everything. He planted his hands on his hips, spread his sneakered feet and cocked his head in a gunman's pose. "Yep," he drawled, his blue eyes gleaming, "I'm here again. Wanna make something of it, pilgrim?"

"Is Brynn here?"

Shane didn't seem to mind that Joe refused to acknowledge his teasing. "She's changing her clothes. We're going bowling."

"You're going bowling?"

"Nothing wrong with your hearing, is there, Doc?"

"Joe?" Brynn stepped up behind Shane, looking surprised. She wore a brightly striped, scoop-neck T-shirt, with denim shorts, white sport socks and sneakers.

Joe's first instinct was to step between Brynn and Shane, putting considerably more distance between this attractive young couple.

"I wasn't expecting to see you today."

Joe nodded. "I know you have plans. I won't keep you. I just stopped by to bring you something."

"Another crystal clock, Doc?" Shane quipped.

Joe was still looking at Brynn when he answered. "It's Quinn Gallagher's newest police mystery. You mentioned to Dad the other day that you like Gallagher's books. I just finished reading this one, and I thought you might enjoy it."

Brynn accepted the package eagerly. "Why, thank you. I've looked forward to reading this. I was going to wait for it to come out in paperback, but now I don't have to be so patient. I'll take very good care of it, I promise."

"Just enjoy it. Books are meant to be read and experienced, not handled with cotton gloves and stored in glass cases."

"You like shoot-'em-up thrillers, Brynn?" Shane asked, sounding surprised.

"Love them. I also love romances, classic British mysteries, some science fiction and fantasy and Garfield comic books. I just love to read."

Shane made a face and pushed a hand through his thick brown hair. "I'm afraid I'm not much of a reader. Can't seem to sit still long enough to concentrate."

"That doesn't surprise me." Brynn smiled at Shane with such comfortable affection that Joe felt his hands begin to clench. He relaxed them quickly, before anyone noticed, and took a step toward the door.

"Have a good time bowling, you two. I'll see you around."

"You're welcome to join us, Doc," Shane said, and he looked completely sincere with the invitation.

"Thanks, Shane, but I have things to do this afternoon."

"Thank you again for the book, Joe. I can't wait to read it."

Joe wasn't thrilled to drive away, leaving Brynn to have fun with Shane. His only hope was that Brynn would think of him now—at least a little—during her afternoon with the younger man.

Chapter Eleven

Brynn neither saw nor heard from Joe again until the following Wednesday. But out of sight, in this case, was most definitely *not* out of mind.

She found herself thinking of all him all the time. While working with his nieces and nephews. Visiting her friend in the hospital where she felt his presence so keenly. Reading the book he'd brought her because he thought she would enjoy it.

All the time.

She wondered if he knew his silence would only make her more aware of him.

When she did see him again, it was the same way he usually came to her—without warning.

It was midafternoon Wednesday. A warm June breeze caressed Brynn's cheek and ruffled her hair as she sat on a lawn swing built for two, baby Justin in her arms. He gazed up at her in slightly cross-eyed fascination as she sang softly to him, gently pushing the swing with her foot.

He was such a beautiful baby. She stroked a finger over his perfectly formed head, with its fuzz of curly black hair. His chubby little cheek was impossibly soft, and his tiny mouth puckered reflexively when her finger strayed close to the corner.

She laughed, interrupting the song she'd been singing. "You couldn't possibly be hungry. You just guzzled down an entire bottle."

"He's growing. Takes a lot of fuel to get from that size to full-grown D'Alessandro male."

Brynn's jerk of reaction startled Justin in turn. Tiny arms flailed, and the baby's mouth opened for a squawk of displeasure. Brynn lifted him quickly to her shoulder and patted his back, looking chidingly at Joe.

"You scared us."

"Sorry. I thought you heard me walk up." He motioned toward the swing beside her. "May I?"

"Of course." She scooted over to give him more room.

The swing jolted when he lowered himself onto it. The seat was just large enough to accommodate them both, his left leg brushing her right.

Joe reached over to stroke his nephew's cheek. "Hey, kid, how's it going?"

Justin grunted in response.

Joe laughed. "I'll take that to mean you're doing okay."

"He's doing very well. Growing so fast. And he's such a good baby. He hardly ever cries."

"And why should he cry? He's got it made. Doting parents. A nice home. A brother and a couple of sisters waiting to play with him. And you for a nanny. What more could a kid ask for?''

Flustered by the warmth in Joe's voice, Brynn concentrated on the baby. "He seems to enjoy being outside. It's a beautiful day, isn't it?''

"Yes. It's especially beautiful here.'' Leaving her to try to decipher his tone, Joe reached over to take the baby from her. "C'mere, *nipote*. Come see your *tio* Giuseppe.''

"Giuseppe? Is that your name?''

Joe tickled the baby's chin. "No. It's Joseph. Giuseppe's simply a family nickname.''

He looked so comfortable, so natural, with the baby. So incredibly sexy...

"Where's everyone else?''

His question brought her abruptly back to the conversation. "Um, Tony took the day off. He and Michelle took the older children to a water park for the day.''

"So it's just you and the kid today, huh?''

"Yes.'' Michelle couldn't resist touching Justin's pumping hand. "Just us.''

"You must be enjoying the peace.''

"It's been a very nice day. But I rather miss the noise.''

"You're crazy about those kids, aren't you?''

Her smile felt soft. "Yes.'' She lowered her head and lifted the baby's hand to her lips. "All of them.''

Joe looked at her intently. "You'll be a wonderful mother, Brynn.''

The words were meant as a compliment. She should have been flattered by them. Instead, she was shattered.

She released the baby's hand and straightened,

crossing her arms over her chest. "No golf game with your father today?"

Joe studied her face a moment before answering, making her worry that he would pursue the painful subject further. Instead, he followed her lead. "We played earlier this morning. Dad likes to hit the greens before it gets too warm."

"Who won?"

"One way or another, Dad always wins."

"Why did you come here today, Joe?" She couldn't wait any longer to ask.

"To see you."

She laced her fingers in her lap, staring at the children's play area. "You seem to be making a habit of that."

Joe nestled the sleepy baby more snugly in his arms, rocking him gently with the motion of the swing. "Yes, I've noticed."

"I'm not complaining. I always enjoy visiting with my friends." She stressed the word slightly, hoping to make it clear that friends were all she and Joe could ever be—if, of course, he had anything more in mind.

"That's nice to hear. One of the reasons I came by is to invite you to a Fourth of July cookout Saturday. Dad practically ordered me to bring you."

His casual tone only confused her more about his motives. She wasn't sure by his wording whether Joe was asking her himself or simply relaying a message on behalf of his father. Either way, it would probably be wisest of her to politely decline. Spending even more time with Joe and his charming family was *not* a good idea.

"You might as well say yes," Joe said when she hesitated. "Pop will just come after you if you don't.

He's decided he wants to see you this weekend. And I just told you that he *always* wins.''

"I'll consider it," Brynn said, compromising.

"Sure. You can let me know tomorrow. I'll call you."

She nodded, thinking she could use the time to come up with a very good excuse for not going.

Joe stood suddenly and very carefully deposited his sleeping nephew into Brynn's arms. His head was very close to Brynn's when he made the exchange. She looked up from the baby to find Joe's mouth only inches from hers.

"See you later, *friend*," he murmured. And then he covered her mouth with his, kissing her thoroughly before drawing away.

He was gone before she remembered how to breathe again.

Brynn told herself she went to the Fourth of July picnic only because she didn't want to disappoint Vinnie. He was such a kind man. He'd been so good to her. It would be rude of her to ignore his kind invitation.

All of which was true but irrelevant. She just couldn't seem to say no to Joe. Which was not a good thing if she intended to follow through on her determination to keep him at a safe distance.

Brynn and Joe arrived at his cousin's suburban Dallas home at almost the same moment as Joe's parents. Vinnie and Carla greeted Brynn with enthusiastic hugs. And then they towed her into a dauntingly large crowd of D'Alessandros, introducing her first to their hosts, Paul and Teresa D'Alessandro, and then to so many others that Brynn finally stopped even trying to remember names.

Tony and Michelle and their children weren't there, having left that morning to spend the holiday weekend in Arkansas with Michelle's sister Lindsay. Michael hadn't been able to make it, either. Vinnie complained loudly that two of his three sons had been too busy to come see their "poor, old Papa." He was generally ignored.

Brynn found it interesting to compare the interaction of the D'Alessandro family with that of the Walker siblings. Unlike the Walkers, who'd known one another as adults for only a little more than ten years and had built their relationships from that point, the D'Alessandro clan had been together forever. They were boisterous, garrulous and emotional. Their conversations were peppered with Italian phrases and flailing hands, and they argued as frequently as they agreed. But the affection between them was so obvious it was almost tangible.

Brynn was as fascinated by them as she was bemused by them.

It was embarrassingly obvious from the beginning that everyone thought she was Joe's date. And this crowd was not reticent about pumping for information.

"Have you and Joe been seeing each other long?" Teresa D'Alessandro asked with friendly curiosity.

"I've known Joe and his family for almost two months," Brynn answered carefully. "We've become acquainted during the time I've worked as nanny for Tony and Michelle's children. Joe and I are just friends."

"Of course you are." Teresa patted Brynn's shoulder. "And you make such a cute couple. Thomas! Don't put ketchup in your cousin's hair. Excuse me, Brynn."

Teresa dashed off to settle the crisis, leaving Brynn

ruefully aware that her neatly worded little speech had resolved nothing.

"It's about time Joe's found himself a nice girl," Vinnie's brother, Salvatore, declared a few minutes later. "Some of these young men can't seem to understand that time won't stand still until they're ready to settle down."

Brynn didn't know what she was supposed to say to that. She looked to Joe for guidance. Apparently, he was so accustomed to his family's bluntness that he was able to shrug it off.

"I really don't think the D'Alessandro name is in any danger of dying out," he murmured wryly, looking around at the four generations of family milling around the large, crowded lawn.

"There can never be enough family," his uncle pronounced firmly.

Joe caught Brynn's hand and pulled her away when Salvatore's attention was suddenly focused elsewhere. "I want to introduce you to someone very special."

Someone else to assume she and Joe were a couple? Brynn sighed, but didn't resist.

The woman Joe wanted her to meet was very old and very tiny. So tiny she was almost lost in the hand-crocheted afghan wrapped around her in her wheelchair, even though the afternoon was quite warm.

"Tia Luisa, may I present my friend Brynn Larkin. Brynn, this is my father's aunt Luisa Sanducci."

Surprising sharp and clear dark eyes studied Brynn intently. "*Piacere,* Brynn."

"She's pleased to meet you," Joe murmured in translation.

His great-aunt shot him a repressive look. "I speak *inglese* perfectly well, Giuseppe."

"Of course you do, *Tia*. But Brynn speaks no Italian."

"Then you will have to teach her, *si?*"

Joe's smile turned mischievous. "We've had one lesson already."

"It's very nice to meet you, Mrs. Sanducci," Brynn said quickly, her first chance to speak.

Those intent dark eyes turned in her direction again. "You've been taking care of Antonio's children." It was clear that Luisa kept abreast of family news.

"Yes. They're such good children. I'm very fond of them."

Luisa nodded her silvery head. "I'm told you're very good with them. *Va bene*. It's good that you like children."

Brynn swallowed. It wasn't hard to see where this was headed.

Luisa waved toward a folding chair set up next to her wheelchair. "Sit down so we can talk. Joseph, bring us lemonade. And take your time."

Joe sent Brynn a thumbs-up sign and obediently disappeared, leaving her to engage in an utterly fascinating conversation with this amazing old woman.

Brynn looked very right among Joe's family. She felt very right at his side. So right, in fact, that Joe found himself fantasizing about having her with him at many family gatherings to come.

He knew his family's matchmaking was causing her discomfort. But she handled it well, with patience, grace and good humor. She had seemed to bond very quickly with Luisa. Another big plus, as far as Joe was concerned, since he adored his great-aunt.

He couldn't help thinking of the term Tony had

quoted from Jared Walker: "outsider syndrome." Jared
had coined the phrase to describe the way a former foster child felt in the midst of a large family. Perhaps
Brynn did have those feelings occasionally during the
course of the day—and Joe could almost pinpoint the
times it affected her—but she was able to mingle successfully anyway. So successfully, in fact, that everyone
was making it very clear to Joe that they approved of
her, and that they thought he would be a fool to let her
get away.

He was beginning to agree with them.

Now all he had to do was convince Brynn that there
was no reason for her to panic every time he got close
to her.

He thought he might be making a little progress in
that direction when he approached her late that afternoon and she actually smiled at him. It wasn't quite the
smile he wanted from her—but it was getting much
closer.

"Your aunt Paula was just telling me about the time
you made your first home run in a baseball game."

Joe groaned. "Not that old story."

"Mmm. It seems you ran so fast to home plate you
left your shoes at third base. After that, everyone called
you 'Shoeless Joe, Jr.'"

"They did until I threatened to do bodily injury to
the next person who dared. It wasn't my fault. I *told*
Dad Michael's shoes were too big for me, but he
wouldn't listen. Michael was going through a growth
spurt and he'd only worn the cleats a few times before
they were too small. Dad didn't want a perfectly good
pair of shoes to go to waste. So, there I was, at what
should have been one of the high points of my young
life, and I ran right out of my hand-me-down shoes."

Brynn chuckled. "You must not have known whether to be more proud or embarrassed."

"Pride won out. Hitting that homer felt awfully good."

"And did you get a new pair of shoes for the next game?"

Joe rolled his eyes. "You know my pop. I wore two pairs of socks for the next game. My feet got so hot my toes almost melted. Dad finally broke down and bought me new shoes when that pair was eaten by the neighbor's rottweiler."

Lifting an eyebrow, Brynn studied Joe's face suspiciously. "They just 'happened' to be eaten by the neighbor's dog?"

"I might have accidentally dropped them over the fence. And I *might* have accidentally smeared leftover gravy on them first."

Brynn laughed. "You haven't changed a bit, have you?"

"He was always a scamp and he still is," Carla pronounced, hearing the end of the story as she and Vinnie approached.

"But it's still not too late for the right woman to reform him," Vinnie added with an arch look at Brynn.

Joe noted that Brynn's smile immediately dimmed. He mentally chided his father for being so tactless. He could excuse the rest of the family, but Vinnie should have known better.

Carla spoke quickly, as if she, too, thought the remark ill-timed. "Vinnie and I are going to the fireworks show at the high-school football stadium tonight. Would you two like to go with us?"

"I love fireworks," Brynn admitted.

Joe smiled at her in approval, relieved that she didn't

seem to be in too great a hurry to bring the day to an end. "So do I. We'd be happy to join you."

It felt good to say 'we.' It felt right. He sincerely hoped it felt the same way to Brynn.

The sky exploded with noise, color and light. Red, blue, green, gold, silver, white. Starbursts, pinwheels, cascades; fountains of light glittered in the night sky, then faded to black.

In the darkened stadium bleachers below, a large crowd oohed and aahed on cue, necks craned, eyes wide in wonder.

Brynn was having trouble concentrating on the show in the sky. The stadium bench was so crowded that she had to sit pressed very close to Joe's side. That was distracting enough. But when he reached out to lace his fingers with hers, holding their linked hands on his knee, it would have taken more than a few fireworks to draw Brynn's attention away.

There was something incredibly romantic about sitting in the darkness holding hands, an unaware crowd around them, the heavens alight with color. Brynn didn't even remember the last time she'd simply held hands with a man; she knew that, whenever it had been, it couldn't possibly have felt this good.

She couldn't lie to herself any longer about the way she felt about Joe D'Alessandro. She had fallen so hard for the guy it was a wonder she didn't have bruises. This wasn't the easy affection she felt for Shane Walker. This was serious. And dangerous. If only…

A particularly awesome display induced the spectators to gasp in delight. Joe squeezed Brynn's hand, causing her to look at him. He was watching her, his face in shadows, his dark eyes glittering, his mouth quirked into an enigmatic smile.

''Enjoying the show?'' he asked, making her wonder if he'd noticed her inattention to the fireworks.

She used the excuse of a particularly noisy explosion to give her a moment to steady her voice. ''It's very impressive.''

''I'm enjoying it.'' Joe tightened his grip on her hand. ''Actually, I can't remember when I've enjoyed anything more.''

Brynn stared up at him and felt a few more metaphorical bruises form as she fell just a little harder. And when Joe lifted her hand to his lips and brushed a fleeting kiss over her knuckles, she felt something give inside her.

Something that might have been her last thread of resistance to him.

Though she knew it was silly, Brynn was acutely aware that the main house was empty when Joe took her home that night. Though she rarely saw the family after her workday ended—they'd made a point of giving her privacy in the guest house—she was generally aware that they were so close to her. Like unseen chaperons, there to keep her from doing anything incredibly foolish.

Brynn was afraid to be alone with Joe, but it wasn't his actions she feared. It was her own mixed-up, painful, ever-deepening feelings for him.

She unlocked her door and looked at him over her shoulder, one hand on the doorknob. ''I had a very nice time today,'' she said, thinking he might take the hint and be on his way.

She should have known better.

He rested a hand on the door frame above her head,

standing so close she could feel the warmth of his body. "Will you ask me to come in?"

She found herself staring at his mouth while she debated her answer. He had a beautiful mouth. But then, Joe was an incredibly attractive man, his striking Italian heritage very clearly defined in his features.

Brynn was painfully aware of her own questionable heritage.

"Brynn?"

Still leaning against the door frame, only inches away from her, he lifted his free hand to brush a strand of hair from her cheek. His fingers lingered, gently cupping the side of her face.

"Ask me in," he urged, his voice going husky.

She wanted to. So badly she trembled. She tried to steel herself with a mental list of all the reasons this was such a bad idea, but she was having trouble remembering them. "I..."

He leaned his head down just far enough to brush her mouth with his. It was like being touched with a live wire. She felt the jolt all the way to the soles of her feet.

"Ask me in, Brynn."

She opened the door. She would ask him in, she decided. But only to tell him that this couldn't go any further.

Joe looked almost smugly satisfied when he closed her front door behind them. The only illumination in the living room came from the small lamp she'd left burning in one corner of the room. Hoping to dispel the intimate mood that soft light fostered, Brynn reached toward the switch for the overhead light.

Joe's hand covered hers before she could flip the switch. "We don't really need that, do we?"

Her fingers curled within his grasp. "Would you like something to drink? I could make coffee…"

He drew her gently toward him. "I'm not thirsty."

"Joe…"

"All you have to do," he said, placing her hands on his shoulders, "is tell me to stop."

Her fingers curled into his shirt. His mouth was so very close to hers. All she would have to do would be to rise on tiptoes and their lips would meet.

"Stop," she whispered.

Joe surprised her by laughing softly. "Are you talking to me, or to yourself?"

He was coming to know her much too well. Brynn glared up at him. "We can't do this."

He traced her lower lip with the pad of his right thumb. "We aren't doing anything. Yet."

Her mouth quivered beneath his touch. "I don't know what you want."

"I want *you*, Brynn. I've wanted you as long as I've known you."

She wished she could be happy to hear those words. But they only made her ache with old, pent-up longings. "It wouldn't work. We couldn't be more mismatched."

He brushed his lips across the tip of her nose. "I think we're very well matched. I grow more convinced of that every time we're together."

She shook her head. "I won't deny that I wish you were right. But I know better."

Joe deliberately traced her mouth with his thumb again. And, again, her lips quivered. "When I touch you, you tremble," he said.

He pulled her close, sliding his arms around her, pressing her full-length against him. "When I hold you, your pulse races. And when I kiss you…"

He brushed his lips over hers, once, and then again.

Her knees weakened, and she clung to his shoulders for support.

"When I kiss you, you melt," he murmured against her lips. "I know these things, because I feel them, too. All I have to do is touch you, and I can't think of anything but you. How can you say we're mismatched?"

It was all she could do to say *anything* at that moment. But she managed to force her voice past the lump in her throat.

"I won't deny that I'm attracted to you. Or that I want you, too. It would serve no purpose for me to deny it when we both know I'd be lying."

Joe's beautiful mouth curved into a smile. "Then there's no problem, is there?"

"Not if all you want is tonight. No strings. No promises."

A quick frown crossed his brow. "I never said that."

"It's all I can offer."

Still holding her close, he studied her face for what seemed like a very long time. She met his gaze evenly, trying to look as if she knew what she was doing.

His frown eased, replaced by a slow, sexy smile that nearly stopped her heart. "Then we should make the most of it, shouldn't we?"

There was something in his eyes, something in his voice, that she didn't quite trust. It was almost as if he was saying one thing but meant something else entirely.

She might have questioned him about it, but he gave her no chance. He lowered his mouth to hers and kissed her until she was barely capable of thought, much less speech. And then he lifted her into his arms and carried her to the bedroom.

Brynn wrapped her arms around Joe's neck and fervently hoped she knew what she was doing.

Chapter Twelve

Brynn quickly discovered one interesting fact about making love with a surgeon. He had very skillful hands.

Almost before she knew what was happening, her blouse and slacks were on the floor beside the bed. Joe wasn't smiling when he looked down at her, sliding his hands very slowly up her sides to cup her breasts through the thin lace of her bra.

"I can't think of anything to say that isn't a cliché," he murmured. "All I can think of is how beautiful you are. How much I want you."

"You don't have to say anything at all," she whispered, lifting her arms to him. "Just kiss me, Joe."

"My pleasure," he murmured, gathering her against him.

But Brynn quickly decided the pleasure was most definitely hers.

It was impossible to be shy with Joe. He was so open

and giving, so generous and encouraging, that Brynn responded instinctively, inhibitions forgotten. She didn't have much experience with this sort of thing, but Joe didn't seem to mind. Or even to notice.

Murmuring in English and Italian, Joe caressed every inch of her body, pleasuring her with his lips and his fingers until she squirmed and gasped beneath him. She would have liked to know what he was saying in the rumbly, sexy voice, but she was afraid to listen too closely. She was trying desperately to keep this strictly physical. To pretend it wasn't permanently changing her life.

It wasn't working. She was desperately in love with this man. And just for tonight, she allowed herself to show him, even though she would never tell him.

She pressed against his shoulders until he rolled onto his back, and then she explored him as thoroughly, as relentlessly, as he'd learned her body. She took her time, savoring the look and feel and taste of his near-perfect physique, taking personal satisfaction from each groan of appreciation she drew from him.

She knew full well that nothing would ever be the same for her after this, no matter how hard she tried to pretend otherwise.

When neither of them could wait any longer, Joe groped impatiently for his slacks, shoved his hand in the pocket and pulled out a couple of small foil packets, which he dumped on the nightstand. Brynn waited eagerly for him to rip open one of the packets and don the contents.

He had come prepared, but she would not allow herself to dwell on what he'd been thinking when he'd slipped those condoms into his pocket that evening. She had been taking birth control pills for several years, but she saw no need to mention that now. When it came to pregnancy, Brynn took absolutely no risks. Tonight, she would allow herself to simply enjoy the pleasure she and Joe gave each other.

She clung to him when he slipped inside her and she rocketed almost immediately to the verge of release. Her fingertips dug into his bare, damp shoulders, and her legs wrapped tightly around his slim hips. His voice was husky in her ear when he whispered something that sounded like "*Ti amo,* Brynn."

It didn't mean what it sounded like, Brynn assured herself as rational thought slipped further away. He was only expressing enjoyment, nothing more.

But the words that echoed in her mind as waves of pleasure carried her into incoherence were much more basic.

I love you, Joe.

Joe slipped back into bed a while later and smiled when he saw that Brynn hadn't moved a muscle during the short time he'd been gone. He brushed a strand of hair away from her face, then pressed a kiss to her temple. He couldn't seem to stop touching her. Kissing her.

Loving her.

She opened her eyes and smiled up at him, the shadows gone for once. "And I thought the fireworks at the football stadium were impressive," she murmured.

He chuckled and kissed the tip of her nose. "Why, thank you, ma'am. I aim to please."

She reached up to touch his cheek. "How can you sound so Italian one minute and so pure-dee-ol' Texan the next?"

"Years of practice."

"However you do it, I like it."

"*Grazie,* darlin'."

Brynn laughed, the sound so pleasantly musical that Joe's throat tightened in response.

"Now, that might be carrying it a little too far," she said.

"I love your laugh," he murmured, running his fingertips over her kiss-darkened mouth as if to capture the sound. "And your smile. You should always look this happy."

He wished he could take the words back when her smile immediately dimmed.

"I'm usually happy," she said, sounding defensive.

He thought of all the times he'd seen painful memories reflected in her eyes. "As long as you're happy now," he replied, his tone conciliatory.

He bent his head to kiss her before she could say anything more, lingering until he felt her soften beneath him again, her hands sliding up his arms to his shoulders.

Several long, spectacular kisses later, Brynn sighed and looked at the clock. "It's getting late. After midnight. Do you have to work in the morning?"

"I'll make rounds at the hospital. But I'm used to getting by without a lot of sleep. It's a talent all doctors develop in med school."

"Still, you need your rest."

"I was sort of hoping you'd ask me to stay over," he said, giving her what he hoped was a charmingly persuasive smile. "Tony and Michelle are out of town, so we have privacy. And I always keep an overnight bag in the trunk of my car, in case I have to shower and change at the hospital."

He could almost see the automatic excuses already forming in Brynn's mind. "I, uh—"

"I'll even make breakfast. I cook a mean stack of pancakes."

"I'm not sure it's such a good idea for you to stay over," Brynn said, not quite meeting his eyes. "I was serious when I said this was just for one night, Joe. We don't want to risk turning it into anything more than it really was."

He felt his eyes narrow. He tried to keep his voice neutral when he asked, "And what was it, really?"

"A, um, temporary aberration."

Joe wondered almost idly how he could be so besotted with Brynn one moment and so annoyed with her the next. "You make it sound as though we just made a big mistake."

"I hope we didn't," she whispered.

"Just what, exactly, do you expect us to do now? Pretend tonight never happened? Go back to being passing acquaintances?"

She was watching him warily now, probably sensing his mounting irritation. "I still consider us friends, of course. Good friends."

Joe tossed off the sheet and reached for his pants. "I suppose I should feel honored."

Brynn struggled to sit up while still holding the sheet to her throat. "You said you understood."

"What is it I'm supposed to understand, Brynn?"

"I tried to tell you I'm not interested in a relationship. Especially not—"

She bit off the words, but it was too late. Joe's temper flared.

Holding his shirt in one fist, he leaned into Brynn's face and trapped her between his arms.

"Especially not with me? Is that what you were going to say?" Unlike most of his relatives, Joe didn't get louder when he got angry. His voice always became very quiet.

She swallowed. "I didn't mean it that way."

"How *did* you mean it?"

Clearing her throat, Brynn tried to scoot sideways on the bed. "I think I should get dressed."

He didn't budge, still holding her between his arms. "What's wrong with me, Brynn? Why is it so impossible for you to imagine having a relationship with me?"

"There's nothing wrong with you. You're practically perfect."

Joe frowned. "Funny, the way you make that sound like an insult."

"I didn't mean to insult you. I'm only being honest. I told you earlier that you and I are mismatched. There's obviously a physical element—after tonight, I can hardly deny that. But there can't be anything more."

"I don't know which of us you're lying to, Brynn, me or yourself. But you *are* lying. What's between us is a hell of a lot more than physical attraction. It has always been more than that. No matter what you say, you'll never convince me you're the type to make love with someone on the basis of no more than physical attraction. I know you better than that."

She looked determinedly at his shoulder. "I'll admit I don't have a lot of experience with lovemaking—as you could probably tell," she added, her cheeks going scarlet. "But—"

"It scared you," he cut in. "We were so damned good together you knew it was more than a fling. So now you're trying to run me off. Well, it's not going to work, Brynn. I'll leave now, if that's what you want.

But I'll be back. And I won't pretend we're nothing more than pals.''

He straightened and pulled his shirt over his head, smoothing it over his jeans with jerky motions. This was not the way he'd wanted the evening to end. He was handling it very badly.

But, damn it, she had hurt him.

Brynn reached for the short, blue satin robe that had been lying across the back of her vanity chair. She donned the garment quickly and tied the belt so tightly it would probably take scissors to loosen it.

Maybe she sensed some of the pain behind his anger. Her voice was softer when she spoke again. "I'm sorry, Joe. Please believe this isn't about you. It's me.''

He sighed and pushed a hand through his tousled hair. "What are we doing? How did we go so quickly from making love to quarreling?"

But he knew what had happened. He'd pushed too hard and too fast. Knowing Brynn's fears—if not the reasons behind them—he had still expected too much from her.

He'd let his heart overrule his head.

"I'm the one who's sorry. I shouldn't have snapped at you. I know you want to go slowly. I guess I'm just not the patient type.''

She frowned and shook her head. "It isn't a matter of patience. Nothing has changed between us. And nothing will.''

"Everything changed tonight, Brynn. I know you're nervous about admitting it now, but we can't go back to the way things were before we made love.''

She paled. "I don't know what you want from me.''

She sounded so confused and forlorn that he couldn't

resist reaching out to touch her cheek, the gesture meant to both comfort and reassure her.

"I think you do know what I want," he murmured. "And that's why you're so scared."

He watched her swallow. Hard. And then he took a step back. "I'll go now. But, Brynn—I *will* be back."

After tonight, he really had no other choice.

Brynn might have slept a total of three hours that night. She felt like a zombie on Sunday, too tired, stressed and confused to even think clearly. She knew she did a lousy job of hiding her jumbled emotions from Kelly during their long visit that afternoon at the hospital. She wasn't sure she was much more successful at concealing them from Tony and Michelle when they returned home late that afternoon.

She hated feeling so moody and withdrawn. It reminded her entirely too much of her mother. And that thought only reminded her of all the reasons she and Joe were wrong for each other. Which only depressed her all over again.

She was beginning to think again that it had been a mistake for her to move to Dallas with Kelly. If Brynn hadn't been driving on that fateful day, maybe there wouldn't have been an accident. Kelly wouldn't have spent over a month in a hospital room. They would never have met the Walkers or D'Alessandros. Brynn would never have known Joe.

She sighed and buried her face in her hands. It was getting late Sunday evening and she had to be up early for her duties with the children. After the little sleep she'd gotten the night before, she knew she needed her rest, but she was almost afraid to go back to the bed she'd shared so briefly with Joe.

What had she been thinking? Had she been so intoxicated by the lovely day she'd spent with him that she'd almost forgotten the vows she'd made to herself during the past few years?

The telephone rang, startling her so badly she jumped. Thinking maybe it would be Michelle or Kelly or Shane—but somehow knowing it was Joe—she lifted the receiver nervously. "Hello?"

"You weren't asleep yet, I hope," Joe said without bothering to identify himself.

She moistened her lips. "No, not yet."

"How are you?"

The simple question seemed to encompass so many levels that Brynn didn't quite know how to answer. She settled for the standard "I'm fine."

"Did Tony and Michelle get home okay?"

"Yes, late this afternoon. The children had a nice time visiting their cousins."

"Did they have any trouble traveling with the baby?"

"Michelle said he was an angel. The only problem they encountered all weekend was when Katie fell and hit her head on something. She has a colorful bruise, but she's fine."

"Tony and Michelle certainly have their hands full. But they seem to enjoy every minute of it."

"They're wonderful parents."

"Tony had two great examples to follow—our mom and dad. I only hope I'm as good a father as Dad and Tony when the time comes. And Michelle was very close to her adoptive parents, though they were a bit smothering and overprotective."

Brynn tried to respond evenly, though Joe's reference to having his own children had made her heart ache.

"After what happened to Michelle as a child, no one could blame her parents for being overprotective."

"What was your mother like, Brynn? You don't talk about her."

Brynn bit her lip, her fingers tightening on the receiver. Maybe it was time to tell Joe about her mother. It would be easier over the telephone because she wouldn't have to see his expression. And he would finally understand why she was so insistent that she was so wrong for a man who valued family above everything else. A man who spoke so easily and so eagerly about the time when he would have children of his own.

"My mother was a very troubled woman. Her own mother had several children, but they were all taken away because of her incompetence to care for them. My mother, Connie, was raised in a series of institutions until she was placed in a home for problem teenagers. It was there she met Danny Smith."

"Your father?"

"That's what she told me. She said Danny was a clown—always making jokes and playing tricks. He made her laugh…and she fell in love with him. By his eighteenth birthday, he was already an alcoholic," she added flatly. "That's why he'd been placed in that particular home. My mother said he was rarely sober the entire year she knew him. But she didn't care. She planned to spend the rest of her life with him. And then he died in a car accident."

"She must have been devastated."

"Yes. She'd had some emotional problems before that—which was why she was placed in the home where she met Danny. But after he died, she was never really stable again, if she ever had been."

"Did she know she was pregnant when he died?"

"No. She found out afterward. From what I've been able to determine, she settled down for a while when I was born, but by the time I was a toddler, she began having problems again. She would leave me with a neighbor, saying she would be back in an hour, and then she wouldn't come back for days. Or she would have wild parties at our apartment or trailer or wherever we were living at the time and the police would come and take me away from her. I would be placed in a foster home until she could convince someone to give her another chance with me. And then she would become so depressed that she wouldn't get out of bed for days. I had to eat whatever I could find in the kitchen—dry cereal, cookies, peanut butter straight from the jar. And I would eventually be taken away again."

"Was your mother ever treated for her problems?"

"She was diagnosed with bipolar disorder. When she was on medication, she was better. Unfortunately, she didn't take her pills very regularly."

"You said she died when you were thirteen?"

"She took a handful of pills with a couple bottles of tequila. I was living in a foster home at the time, so I was spared being the one to find her."

"I'm sorry, Brynn." And then he stopped and exhaled in frustration. "That sounded inadequate, didn't it? I don't really know what else to say."

"You don't have to say anything. I only told you about my past so you would understand."

"Understand what?"

She swallowed. "Why I said you and I are mismatched."

The line was silent for a moment. And then Joe said, "No. I still don't understand that."

Brynn shook her head in disbelief. "Weren't you

even listening? We couldn't be more different. You came from a comfortable, white-collar, happy two-parent family. My only family was a mother who couldn't take care of herself, much less me. You're a doctor, a surgeon. I'm a nanny."

"None of which makes the least bit of difference to me. I know the person you've become, Brynn. And I admire you very much for having the fortitude to overcome all those obstacles and make a real life for yourself."

She ran a hand through her hair, resisting the impulse to pull. "I didn't tell you about my childhood to make you admire me."

"I already admired you. Now I only admire you more."

"Joe, you're being deliberately obtuse."

"I'm not trying to be. I simply don't understand the problem. Yes, our backgrounds are very different. But we've got plenty in common now. I think we've proven that."

Memories of their lovemaking filled her head, making her face heat and her skin tingle. She closed her eyes, but that only made the images clearer in her mind. She opened them quickly, focusing on the crystal clock on her bookcase. The clock Joe had bought her as a housewarming gift.

"Do you want an affair, Joe? Is that it? Some great sex, with no strings, no expectations?"

Her blunt question seemed to take him aback. "You know me better than that."

"Yes," she said a bit sadly. "I do."

"My feelings for you are more than lust. More than temporary. And I have expectations, Brynn. A lot of them."

She sighed. "Before you start thinking too far ahead, you should probably understand a few more things about me. I want to finish college. I plan to enroll in evening classes as soon as possible. I want to teach on the elementary school level. I'm at least three years away from that goal, but it's what I plan to be doing before I'm thirty. And once I enroll in classes for the fall, I'll have very little free time when I'm not working for Michelle and Tony."

"I think…"

"What I *don't* plan to do is have children of my own," she continued doggedly. "Ever."

The silence that followed that emphatic statement was long and deep. "Why?" Joe asked finally, simply.

"Why do you think? My mother was mentally ill. *Her* mother was mentally ill. My father was a teenage alcoholic. Do you really think I would choose to create a child with that genetic heritage?"

"No one knows exactly how their children will turn out, Brynn. Michelle's biological father was an alcoholic, and her mother died of poor health before she was thirty. Michelle knew nothing more about her genetic history. And yet she and Tony have taken that particular risk four times…very successfully, so far. Michelle's siblings have all chosen to have children, as well. And they've all been blessed with healthy offspring. Genetics is a crapshoot, still heatedly debated in the medical community. There are no guarantees—for anyone."

Brynn couldn't compare herself with Michelle or with anyone else. She had to deal with her own fears—and this was the solution she'd chosen long ago.

"It's getting late," she said, her throat tight. "I have to go."

"Brynn, we need to talk."

"I think we've talked enough tonight. I won't change my mind—I can't. This is the way it has to be for me. And I know it isn't what you want. So let's just say good night, Joe. Please."

She hung up quickly, not even giving him a chance to bid her good-night in return.

Okay, she'd been a coward. She'd stated the facts, then hung up on him. Maybe she'd just become overwhelmed with emotion at having to bare so much of herself to him—her past, her fears, her most intimate decisions. She simply hadn't been willing to get into a more detailed discussion.

Joe didn't try to call her back. She imagined that he was busy thinking about what she'd told him. Once he'd had time to reflect, she knew he would agree that it would be best to end their affair now. Before anyone was hurt. He would understand there was no future for them.

She wondered if that inescapable reality was even half as painful for him as it was for her.

Chapter Thirteen

Monday was a long, busy day for Brynn. She'd slept fitfully after her conversation with Joe, so she started the day tired. The children were still a bit wired from their weekend trip, making them more fussy and boisterous than usual. Brynn had to struggle to keep them occupied and out of trouble all day, an especially difficult undertaking because she had all four children in her care during the afternoon, when Michelle had to attend a board meeting.

By the time Michelle returned home to take the children off her hands, Brynn was completely drained. She didn't even make a trip to the hospital, settling, instead, for a long telephone visit with Kelly.

Unlike Brynn, Kelly was in a very good mood. "Dr. Joe came to see me this afternoon."

Brynn forced herself to speak evenly. "Did he?"

"Yes. He's letting me leave the hospital later this

week! I'll be in a wheelchair for a little while, then on crutches for several weeks, and I'll have to come back nearly every day for physical therapy, but I'll be out of this place.''

"That's wonderful," Brynn said, and meant it. She looked forward to having Kelly with her in the little guest house. She wanted to watch for herself as Kelly got stronger and back to her former active self. And she would welcome the companionship during the long evenings Brynn would otherwise spend thinking about Joe.

Evenings like the one that stretched ahead of her.

Less than half an hour after Brynn and Kelly concluded their telephone visit, someone knocked on the front door. Brynn glanced at her watch, noting that it was just after seven. Drawing a deep breath, she opened the door. Her nervous frown turned to a smile when she saw who stood on her doorstep.

"Shane. What on earth...?"

"Quick. Grab something."

She reached out to relieve him of some of the many packages balanced precariously in his arms. "Is that better?"

He gave her one of his wicked, flashing smiles. "Well, I was hoping you'd grab me, but that'll do, I guess."

"Shut up and come in," she told him with mock severity.

"That's why I like visiting you, Brynn. You're always so gracious and welcoming."

Shane dumped the remainder of the packages on the coffee table. He extracted one and handed it to Brynn. "For you, ma'am."

She dug in the bag and pulled out a delightfully goofy-looking purple beanbag monkey. She couldn't help but return its engaging smile. "How cute. Thank you."

"You're welcome. Now let's open the rest of this stuff."

Curiously, she walked closer as Shane began to rummage through bags. He pulled out food: peanut butter-and-jelly sandwiches, raw carrots, grapes and store-bought chocolate chip cookies. Comfort food, he explained, his grin as goofy as the purple monkey's.

"I hope you haven't eaten yet," he added.

"No." She looked at the feast spread on her table and giggled. "I'll get us sodas."

Shane stopped her with an upraised hand. "No need. I've taken care of everything."

He pulled out a bottle of expensive red wine. "They say this tastes best at room temperature. Hope it goes well with PB and J."

Brynn laughed. "You're insane."

"So I've been told. Sit down. No, not on the couch, on the floor. Kick off your shoes—get comfortable."

She obliged. "Now what?"

He dug out a stack of videos. "Call this dinner theater. We'll be entertained while we eat."

"What movies did you bring?"

He held them up one at a time, naming each. "*Jumanji. Men in Black. Mouse Hunt.*"

She blinked. "Um—"

"I raided Molly's video collection. All I had were shoot-'em-ups in mine, and we needed silly stuff tonight."

"Why do we need silly stuff tonight?" she asked patiently, accepting a sandwich when he handed it to her.

"Because," he said, settling cross-legged on the carpet beside her and reaching for the food, "you need cheering up. Kelly said so."

"Kelly said so?" she parroted blankly.

"Yeah. I went to see her this afternoon. She said you were feeling kind of down and needed cheering up. So, here I am. What movie do you want to see first?"

Brynn realized how little chance she'd ever had of hiding her feelings from Kelly, who had always known her too well.

"You choose," she answered. "I haven't seen any of them."

Shane laughed. "Darlin', you are in for a treat."

Brynn licked a smear of peanut butter from her finger while Shane popped a video in the player. He was reaching for the remote when she placed her hand on his arm. "Shane?"

"Yeah?"

"You're a good friend."

His dimples deepened. "That the nicest thing anyone has said to me in a long time."

Brynn and Shane watched only one of the videos, and they talked so much during it that Brynn hardly knew what the film was about. Their conversation wasn't particularly deep or meaningful; mostly they joked and teased and chattered about inconsequentials.

Neither of them mentioned Joe D'Alessandro.

It was exactly what Brynn needed.

They talked about movies and music and high-school memories, and somehow they ended up looking at an old photo album containing numerous pictures of Brynn and Kelly as teenagers in Mrs. Fendel's foster home.

"There are quite a few photos in here," Shane commented, flipping through page after page of snapshots of the two best friends in dozens of poses. "A lot more than I have of myself as a kid."

"Mrs. Fendel wanted us to have memories of our youth. She tried very hard to give us as normal a life as possible, though she never pretended to be our mother. She was a dedicated and very efficient caretaker who expected a great deal from us and then worked very hard to help us live up to her expectations."

"Sounds like you were pretty lucky to have her, considering," Shane murmured, looking at a photo of thin, angular, well-intentioned Mrs. Fendel.

"Yes. She was a good guardian. I owe a lot to her."

An age-yellowed snapshot fell out of the back of the album when Shane closed the book. He picked it up and glanced at it. "Who are these people?"

Brynn knew her smile had vanished. "My parents. That was taken the day my father died in a car accident later that evening. It was his eighteenth birthday. My mother's pregnant in the photo, though she wasn't showing yet. That's the only photograph I have of either of them."

Shane examined the old snapshot intently. "You look exactly like your mother."

Being compared with her mother always made Brynn shiver. "I know."

"But you have your father's eyes, I think. That pale, clear blue..." He fell silent, holding the photograph closer, suddenly frowning.

She wondered what had caught his attention. "What is it?"

"You said your father died in a car accident on his eighteenth birthday?"

"Yes. Only hours after that photo was taken."

"Where?"

"Just outside of Longview."

Shane didn't take his eyes off the picture. "And what did you say his name was?"

"Danny Smith. I don't know if that was his birth name. My mother didn't seem to know, either. She simply called him 'Danny.'"

Very slowly, Shane looked up from the picture. He studied Brynn's face as closely as he had the snapshot.

Self-conscious now, she squirmed on the carpet. "What's wrong, Shane?"

He shook his head. "Nothing." He glanced at his watch. "Gosh, it's getting late. I'd better go."

She looked at the clock on the bookshelf. Shane had been there almost three hours, and he still had a long drive ahead of him.

She walked him to the door. "Thank you for coming by, Shane. I really enjoyed the visit."

He patted her cheek in a brotherly fashion. "Are you all cheered up now?"

"Much more so," she assured him.

"Good. Call me any time you need mindless diversion, you hear? I seem to excel at that."

A moment later he was gone, leaving Brynn smiling as she closed the door behind him.

Her smile faded as she picked up the photo album to place it back on the bookshelf where she usually kept it. What was it about the photograph of her parents that had so captured Shane's attention? Had he seen more than a physical resemblance between Brynn and her mother? Or was that only her old paranoia showing?

She turned off the lights in the living room and walked into the bedroom. As she dressed for bed, she found her thoughts turning to Joe, though she'd been able to avoid thinking of him, for the most part, while Shane was there to distract her.

Joe hadn't called. She hadn't been aware, until now, that she'd more than half expected him to. Apparently, her tale of her sordid background and plans for her future had made him rethink his interest in her. She expected him to be polite about it, knowing Joe and his impeccable manners. But he would allow their short-lived romance to end now.

He would see that there was really no other option for them.

Brynn had agreed to take Jason, Carly and Katie to a pizza parlor-arcade for lunch Wednesday. Michelle, who was keeping the baby home with her while she caught up on paperwork, suggested Brynn take the minivan for the outing, so she wouldn't have to transfer booster seats to her car. Brynn was just loading her charges into the van when an all-too-familiar sports car turned into the driveway.

Brynn swallowed hard, then pasted on a smile that must have looked fake, since Joe nearly grimaced when he saw it. Spotting their uncle, the children tumbled back out of the van.

"Dr. Joe! Dr. Joe!" They threw themselves at him. He knelt and caught them deftly in his arms for a group hug.

He looked over their heads at Brynn. "Hello, Brynn."

"Hi, Joe."

"I came to visit the little monsters. Are you just getting home with them or just leaving?"

"Just leaving. I promised to take them to Pizza 'n' Prizes for lunch."

"Come with us, Dr. Joe," Jason urged eagerly. "I'll beat you at air hockey."

"In your dreams you'd beat me," Joe retorted, ruffling the boy's dark hair.

"Come with us, Dr. Joe," Carly repeated, clutching Joe's hand. "You always win lots of tickets for us."

"Well, I *am* free for the afternoon. But maybe you should ask your nanny if she minds having another kid along to watch out for."

Katie giggled. "You're not a kid, Dr. Joe. You're a grown-up."

"There are some who might disagree with you there. So, what do you say, Brynn? Can I go, too? Please, please?"

Brynn found herself suddenly the focus of three pairs of young, pleading eyes and one pair of totally shameless, full-grown male eyes.

"You're welcome to come with us," she said, because there was really nothing else to say.

"Great. You put the kids in the van, and I'll run inside and tell Michelle what's going on, so she'll know why my car's parked in her driveway."

Even more excited now about the outing, the children practically bounced in their seats, making it even more difficult than usual for Brynn to get them safely buckled in. She couldn't imagine why Joe had decided to accompany them. Had he simply wanted to spend time with his nephew and nieces—or was there more to it than that?

Maybe this was his way of putting their relationship back on a "just friends" basis.

She tried to analyze his behavior toward her during lunch. He seemed comfortable enough with her, laughing frequently, talking as easily to her as to the children.

He helped her persuade the impatient girls to eat before playing in the arcade, and then he proved very helpful watching them in the crowded, noisy game room.

They must look like a family to the others in the place, Brynn couldn't help thinking. Tony's children resembled Joe enough to be his own; gazing into their big, dark D'Alessandro eyes, Brynn could easily imagine a child of Joe's. Too easily, actually. The image made her heart ache.

He would be such a good father. He was so tender and patient with the children. He indulged them shamelessly but was able to be firm when they threatened to get out of hand. He reminded her very much of his own father—and she couldn't imagine a more worthy role model than Vinnie D'Alessandro.

By the time Brynn announced that they had to go, Joe and the children had won a significant stack of tickets from the arcade games. The children divided the tickets evenly among them, then spent a long time deliberating between the cheap prizes available for "purchase" with the tickets.

Joe laughed at Katie's fierce frown of concentration. "It isn't a life or death decision, Katie. Just pick something."

"But I want it to be the *right* something, Dr. Joe," Katie told him earnestly.

"Oh. Of course." He appeared properly chastened.

Brynn finally had to speak firmly, or they might have been there for the rest of the day. "We really have to go now. Make your selection, Katie. Jason, Carly, do you know what you want?"

Their hands filled with plastic toys worth perhaps a fifth of what they'd spent to win them, the satisfied trio piled into the van. Brynn and Joe made sure they were buckled in, then took them home.

Her work finished, Michelle was waiting to hear all about the outing. Joe spoke over the children's enthusiastic chattering. "Are you finished with Brynn for a while?" he asked Michelle.

"For the rest of the day, actually," Michelle replied, smiling knowingly at Brynn. "I've finished my work, and I promised the kids we'd watch their new video this afternoon."

"Great. Brynn, since you're free, I'll take you up on that coffee you offered."

She hadn't offered coffee, of course. But she could hardly say so with everyone watching them.

"We have coffee here, Dr. Joe," Carly commented.

"Why don't you go put your things away and get the video ready, Carly," Michelle said quickly. "I'm sure Dr. Joe and Brynn will enjoy a little time to rest after wrangling you three most of the afternoon."

There seemed to be no getting out of this, Brynn thought as she and Joe walked in silence to the guest house. It had been easy enough to spend time with Joe, to simply enjoy being with him, as long as the children had been there to distract them from their personal issues. But now they were alone again, for the first time since that frankly revealing telephone conversation, and Brynn was having a very difficult time not thinking about the last time they were alone together—in her bedroom.

She reminded herself that Joe's manner had been nothing more than casually friendly all afternoon. He hadn't even touched her; he had actually seemed to go out of his way to avoid touching her. He probably just wanted to talk.

They walked into her living room and closed the door behind them. Brynn turned to say something—she didn't know what, exactly—but before she could speak, she found herself mashed between the door and Joe's body, her mouth crushed beneath his.

Acting solely on instinct, she wrapped her arms around his neck and kissed him back.

It had only been a few days since they'd kissed, but Brynn felt as if she'd been starving for him and hadn't realized it. All the self lectures, all the mental arguments and denials, had apparently accomplished nothing. She couldn't simply stop loving Joe just because she knew she should.

Was it possible that he felt at least a bit the same way?

Joe lifted his mouth just long enough to murmur, "I've missed you, Brynn." And then he kissed her again.

His hands raced over her, reminding them both of the pleasure their bodies had found together before. Brynn gasped into his mouth when he clutched her hips and pressed her intimately against him, letting her know that he was as aroused as she was.

Every nerve ending in her body tingled. She wanted him so badly she could hardly stand upright, which made her have to cling to him for support.

If this was all they could have, it was still spectacular.

Joe pressed his lips to her cheeks, her forehead, her chin, the tip of her nose. And then he pulled her close and simply held her. "You missed me, too," he said, sounding both pleased and relieved.

"Yes," she said, because it would be foolish to deny it when she was plastered all over him, clinging to him as if her life depended on him.

"I gave you some space because you seemed to want it, but I couldn't stay away any longer. All I could think about was how badly I wanted to be with you."

She buried her face in his shoulder, an enormous lump forming in her throat. It had been hard enough to resist him over the telephone; it was impossible when she was being held in his arms, hearing him tell her how he'd missed her.

Maybe Joe had decided that this was enough for him. That he could be content, for now, with what she had to offer—herself, and nothing more.

"Remember that coffee we were going to have?" he murmured against her mouth.

She traced the line of his jaw and nibbled a kiss on his lower lip. "You want me to make some now?"

"Actually, I've decided it's too hot for coffee. Much too hot," he added, lifting her onto her tiptoes and sliding his hands around to cup her bottom.

"Definitely too hot," she agreed breathlessly.

He tugged at the hem of the red knit top she'd worn with khaki slacks. "Maybe we would cool off if we get rid of some of these clothes."

Brynn gulped. "Or maybe we'd just get hotter."

Joe's flashing white grin was the embodiment of wicked mischief. "I guess that's a risk we'll just have to take."

It had been nighttime when Brynn and Joe had made love before. They'd been alone on the estate, with no risk of interruption. It had been the most romantic night of Brynn's life.

This time it was midafternoon. The July sun slanted through the bedroom windows, making the room bright and warm. Michelle and the children were in the house just next door. The telephone or doorbell could ring at any time.

But it was still incredibly romantic.

When the last broken sigh had faded away, and the husky groans of satisfaction were silenced, Brynn lay limply on Joe's shoulder, trying to recover enough strength to move. This, she thought ruefully, was no way to end an ill-fated relationship.

Joe lifted his left arm—making it seem like a major undertaking—and looked at his watch. "I have to go," he said reluctantly. "I have an appointment at five."

Which didn't give them time for a serious talk, Brynn realized with a glance at the clock. "You'd better hurry, or you'll be late."

He sighed deeply. "I'd rather stay here, with you."

There was nothing she would have liked more than to keep him in her bed for the rest of the day. And night. For the rest of the week, for that matter. But she had to face reality occasionally. She pushed herself upright and reached for her clothes.

Fifteen minutes later, she stood at the front door to see Joe off. They'd dressed quickly, and Brynn still felt a bit disheveled. She ran a hand through her hair as she looked up at Joe, not quite certain what to say.

He leaned his head down to kiss her. "I'll call you later."

"All right."

"I enjoyed spending the day with you."

"So did I," she admitted.

He touched her cheek and smiled tenderly down at her. "Did you really think you'd scared me off?"

"I, er—"

"You should know me better by now. I don't scare

so easily. I'm here for the duration, Brynn. Get used to it.''

While she was still trying to think of something to say, he kissed her again, then slipped out the front door, closing it quietly behind him.

Brynn staggered to the couch and collapsed onto it, her legs suddenly too shaky to support her. She supposed there was no denying now that she was having an affair with Dr. Joe D'Alessandro.

Joe had made it quite clear that he would be back. *''I'm here for the duration,''* he had said. That made it sound as though he was thinking in terms of much more than an affair. His words implied permanence. Commitment.

Hadn't he listened to a thing she'd told him over the telephone? Did he really want to tie himself to the daughter of a deeply disturbed woman? Someone who could make no guarantees of her own future stability, based on what she knew of her parents—much less take a chance of passing her genes on to offspring?

Did Joe, with his family-worshiping, Italian Catholic background, his great-aunt who'd already named his first son, his parents who made no secret that they wanted more grandchildren, really think he could be content with a decision to have no children of his own?

Her doorbell chimed. Apparently, Joe had come back sooner than she'd expected. Had he forgotten something?

She rose and opened the door. "Did you...?"

Her voice faded. There was a man on her doorstep, but it wasn't Joe D'Alessandro. It was one of the Walker twins. One of the private investigators who worked for Tony.

Why on earth had he come to see *her?*

"Hello, Brynn. I hope this isn't an inconvenient time for you."

She wasn't sure whether he was Ryan or Joe Walker. She settled for a noncommittal, "Not at all. Come in, Mr. Walker."

"'Ryan,'" he supplied helpfully, stepping past her. "I suppose you haven't been around us enough yet to tell us apart."

"I wouldn't think many people can tell you apart."

"I'll give you a clue. I have a scar in my right eyebrow. Joe doesn't."

She looked at the thin white line that bisected his eyebrow and extended onto his forehead. "Thank you. I'll try to remember that."

Although she couldn't imagine why he'd called on her, Brynn fell back on the manners Mrs. Fendel had drilled into her. "Can I get you something to drink? Soda? Iced tea?"

He shook his head. "No, thank you. I have a couple of questions I'd like to ask you, if you have time."

Brynn sat on the edge of a chair facing the one Ryan had selected. "What questions?"

"First, I need to tell you something about my family. You probably know that we were separated as children, after our parents died."

Though it wasn't a question, she nodded.

"Jared was eleven, Layla was ten, our brother Miles was eight, Joe and I were almost six, Michelle was two and Lindsay was just a baby. Michelle and Lindsay were adopted; the rest of us grew up in foster homes."

She nodded again, wondering where he was leading. "I, um, heard your brother Miles died before the rest of you were reunited."

Ryan took a deep breath. "Yes. Miles Daniel Walker

died in a car accident in Longview some twenty-six years ago. It was his eighteenth birthday, and he and his friends had been drinking beer to celebrate. He and two of his buddies died in the accident. A young woman survived."

Brynn knew she'd gone pale. Her voice came out as little more than a whisper. "My father died in a car accident in Longview. On his eighteenth birthday."

"Yes, I know. Shane told me."

Understanding now where the conversation was going, Brynn shook her head. "Sadly, teenagers die in car accidents all the time, often with alcohol as a contributing factor. My father's name was Danny Smith."

"My brother's middle name was Daniel. My full name is Robert Ryan, and I was called 'Bobby' until I decided I liked my middle name better."

"But you kept your real last name."

He shook his head. "I didn't call myself 'Ryan Walker' from the time I was sixteen until I was reunited with my family ten years ago."

Brynn felt as if something heavy was sitting on her chest, making breathing difficult. "I really don't think..."

Ryan spoke gently when her voice lodged in her throat. "Shane came to my office today. He said he saw a photograph of your father the other day, and it has been bothering him ever since. He thought the photo looked a lot like the only one we have of Miles. And when you told him how your father died, he realized that the coincidences were simply too powerful to ignore. Since he wasn't sure you would want us prying into your past without permission, he insisted I talk to you before I mentioned this to anyone else."

"Are you really suggesting that I could be...?"

"My niece?" he filled in when she stumbled. "I think it's a definite possibility, from what Shane told me."

Brynn's head was spinning. This day had been one shock after another, from Joe's unexpected participation in the pizza outing to the passionate lovemaking that had followed—and now this.

"Would you mind showing me the photo of your father?" Ryan asked. His manner was still calm and relaxed, but Brynn sensed an eagerness in him he couldn't entirely hide.

For a few moments, she was almost immobilized by emotions she couldn't have defined if she'd tried. She was more than half-afraid to show him the snapshot. She didn't know whether she was more worried that he would recognize her father or that he would not.

Her hands were shaking visibly when she handed him the old snapshot. Ryan gave her an encouraging smile before turning his attention to the photograph.

Brynn watched him as he studied it. She saw a muscle work in his jaw.

"Well?" she asked impatiently. "Does he look like your brother?"

Rather than answering, Ryan reached into the inner pocket of the loose sport coat he wore with chinos and an oxford shirt. He pulled out a small brown envelope, which he offered to Brynn.

She noted that his fingers weren't quite steady, either.

She swallowed and opened the envelope, sliding out a photograph that was even older than the one he held. This was a posed, studio shot of a weary-looking woman surrounded by children.

Brynn spotted Jared Walker immediately; he hadn't changed much since childhood, she thought dazedly. A girl who looked much like Layla stood beside Jared, and twin boys and a toddler girl were posed on either side of their mother, who held a baby girl in her lap.

She finally found the courage to look at the last young face. It was a boy with freckled cheeks and sandy hair, and a broad, irrepressible-looking grin. Though this boy was at least ten years younger than the Danny Smith in Brynn's snapshot, the similarities were so pronounced that she knew immediately why Shane had gone to Ryan.

She lifted her eyes slowly, tears threatening. "I—"

Ryan rose and slipped a supportive arm around her shoulders when she choked. "I'd like to look into this, if you don't mind. I hope to find confirmation before we say anything to the others."

She nodded mutely. Even the possibility that she was related to the Walker family made her ache with mingled longing and anxiety.

"It shouldn't take me long to find something," Ryan added. "Try not to think about it, okay?"

She stared at him in disbelief. "How can I *not* think about it?"

He grimaced. "You're right. That was a dumb thing to say. I just don't want you to worry."

"I'll try. But I feel as though my whole world just tilted off its axis," she admitted. "I've been so accustomed to thinking of myself without a family. Now just the possibility that I have aunts, uncles and cousins— well, it's overwhelming."

"Trust me. I understand completely." Ryan's smile was rueful. "When Joe and I first found out our brother and sisters were looking for us, our first instinct was to run. We weren't at all sure we wanted to deal with the entanglements of family after being on our own for so long.

"It was even harder for Joe," he added. "He's always taken things more seriously than I do. He met Lauren at about the same time we found out about our siblings, and he resisted getting involved with her, as well, even though he'd fallen hard for her. After a lifetime of accepting being alone, it's easier not to open your heart to potential disappointment or disillusion."

"You *do* understand," she murmured, blinking back the tears she refused to shed in front of him.

"Yes. But, Brynn, my brother and I found out that family is worth any risk."

"I'm still not convinced that my father was Miles Walker," she insisted, refusing to allow herself to hope without more evidence. "It would just be too bizarre a coincidence that I'm here now, working for Michelle. Things like that just don't happen."

"Things like that happen all the time," Ryan corrected her with a smile. "Don't you ever watch talk shows?"

His expression then grew more serious. "All my siblings would tell you that there have been times we felt that a force we couldn't explain drew us back together. Layla—the fanciful one in our clan—likes to believe our mother and Miles had something to do with it. That they wanted us to be together again. You've met Layla. None of us has the heart to argue with her. And who knows? Maybe she's right."

But Brynn was still reluctant to hope too much. Her past hadn't given her reason to be overly optimistic. "I need proof, Ryan. Paperwork, blood tests, whatever it takes. And then we'll talk again. In the meantime, I don't want anyone else to know about this, all right?"

"It will be our secret," he promised. "And Shane won't say anything, either. But, Brynn…"

"Yes?"

He squeezed her shoulders before stepping away. "When we find our proof, I'll be the first to welcome you to the family."

Chapter Fourteen

Kelly left the hospital the next day. Brynn didn't have to try to collect her alone—Tony, Jared and Shane all volunteered to help. They took Tony's van, so there would be plenty of room for Kelly's wheelchair and the things she'd needed for her six-week stay in the hospital.

Kelly was so excited to leave the hospital she was practically bouncing in her chair. "Gosh, it's hot out. Summer really set in while I was cooped up in this place, didn't it? I can't wait to see our house, Brynn. Oh, did you remember to pack my hairbrush? Careful, Shane, don't drop that plant. The container is breakable."

Everyone was amused by Kelly's babbling. She gave them no time to answer her questions before asking a dozen more. "Nice van, Tony. Jared, do you have my suitcase? Oh, good. Brynn, are you sure you got everything?''

"I'm sure," Brynn said with a laugh. "Will you calm down?''

"I can't help it. I'm so glad to be leaving this place. Even if I have to come back every day for therapy, it will be so wonderful to sleep on a real bed. And eat real food.''

"Cheeseburgers?" Shane suggested.

"Pizza," she put in.

"Fried chicken.''

"Tacos and cheese dip.''

"Hot dogs and chips.''

"Milk shakes," she said with a sigh.

Brynn couldn't help laughing. "If that's all you're going to eat, I'll never be able to help you in and out of that chair.''

"Speaking of which," Tony said as they all paused beside his van, "there is no lift on this van. We'll have to get you inside another way, Kelly.''

Shane stepped forward. "I'll get one side, Dad. You take the other.''

Kelly looked at them doubtfully.

Shane grinned and chucked her chin with his knuckles. "Trust us. We pick up little heifers all the time.''

"Oh, *that* makes me feel better.''

Brynn stood back out of the way as Shane and Jared skillfully transferred Kelly from the wheelchair to her seat in the van. Shane and Kelly were laughing, and even Jared chuckled at their foolishness. Tony stood close by, grinning, ready to help if needed.

As she watched them, Brynn couldn't help thinking that this could be her family. Her uncles. Her cousin. These wonderful, kind, generous and handsome men.

Her heart swelled, but she tried to ignore the feeling. She refused to allow herself to start thinking in terms of family when she'd been so alone for so long. Until she had concrete proof, she would think of them only as her friends.

She couldn't help wondering how they would feel if Ryan produced that proof. Though Ryan had assured her she would be welcomed, past experience had left her wary of high expectations. What if they thought of her as an interloper? An opportunist? What if they didn't believe that it was only coincidence that had brought her into their circles?

Joe came out of the hospital to see Kelly off. He smiled at Brynn, then checked to make sure Kelly was securely fastened into her seat, her legs adequately supported.

Brynn watched him broodingly, wondering—not for the first time—what Joe would think when—or if—he discovered that Brynn was Miles Walker's illegitimate daughter. She knew he would think she should have already discussed this with him, but she simply hadn't known how to bring it up. Would he be annoyed with her for keeping her conversation with Ryan secret for now? Would he feel differently about her if she was, indeed, his sister-in-law's niece? Would knowing the truth strengthen the bond she had formed with Joe and with all the other Walkers and D'Alessandros—or threaten it?

Joe reached out a hand to help Brynn into the van. "I'll be seeing you later," he murmured, giving her hand a discreetly intimate squeeze.

She swallowed hard before nodding and climbing quickly into the vehicle.

Michelle and Cassie waited to greet Kelly and welcome her to her new home. They even had snacks and chilled beverages waiting, creating an impromptu party in the main house. Before the afternoon was over, Vinnie and Carla had dropped by, and Layla, Kevin and Brittany Samples popped in.

Kelly thrived as the center of attention. Without a trace of complaint or self-pity, she sat in her wheelchair, her right leg immobilized in front of her. The clean break in her left leg had healed, but it would be several weeks yet before the crushed bones in her right leg, now held together with pins and rods, would comfortably support her weight.

"She's a trooper, isn't she?" Shane asked in a murmur, catching Brynn alone for a moment in a quiet corner of Michelle's den.

"Kelly's always been very good at making the most of her circumstances," Brynn agreed. "She's never been a whiner."

Shane draped a companionable arm across Brynn's shoulders. "That seems to be something else you and Kelly have in common."

Brynn smiled up at him, unable to suppress a quick wave of affection, and wishing his words were true. Unlike Kelly, she'd always been a worrier. For example, she was terrified that Ryan Walker would return with proof that there was no relationship between Brynn and his family, leaving her alone again after giving her reason to hope.

Though Michelle's den was filled with people— Kelly, Tony and Michelle and their children, Vinnie and Carla, Kevin and Layla and Brittany, Jared, Cassie and Molly—Joe spotted Brynn the moment he entered. She stood in one corner of the room, looking relaxed and contented. That, in itself, shouldn't have annoyed Joe. The fact that she looked so happy while standing within the circle of Shane Walker's right arm made him absolutely furious.

His first thought was that she certainly wouldn't have looked so comfortable if *he* had put his arm around her right in front of everyone. His second thought was that he really couldn't stand here just looking at them like this. He needed to do something.

Waving acknowledgments to the greetings sent his way, he headed without pausing to the far side of the room. Brynn spotted him…and her smile dimmed. Which only made him angrier, an emotion he hid behind a pleasant expression.

"Hello, Shane," he said, extending his right hand.

Though he looked a bit surprised, since they didn't usually shake hands each time they saw each other, Shane removed his right arm from Brynn's shoulders and took Joe's hand. "How's it going, Doc?"

Satisfied that he'd accomplished what he'd intended, Joe replaced Shane's arm with his own, drawing Brynn to his side. "Hi, darlin'," he said, and kissed her before she could answer.

He was tired of hiding his feelings, tired of trying to make everyone believe that he and Brynn were just pals. They were lovers. He was in love with her. And even if it meant taking the risk of losing her, he couldn't pretend any longer.

Well aware that he'd gotten Brynn's attention—as well as that of everyone else in the room—he lifted his head and deliberately turned his attention away from her, as if the brief kiss of greeting had been a commonplace occurrence for him.

He smiled at Kelly, who was watching his with a

gleam of speculative amusement in her green eyes. "I see you've successfully escaped the hospital. Any problems?"

"None at all," she said airily, though he suspected she was in some discomfort from the activities of the afternoon. "Everyone's taking very good care of me."

Joe felt Brynn trying to inch away from him. He tightened his arm, holding her in place. She would probably give him hell later, but he'd deal with that then. Sometimes it was just too hard to be a sensitive, understanding male. Especially when he'd just seen the woman he loved standing in the arms of another man.

"Kelly's starting to look tired," she said, trying a new tactic. "I should take her to the guest house to rest."

"I'll wheel her over when she's ready," Shane volunteered. "I want to see how fast I can make that buggy go."

Kelly's eyes widened in mock dismay. "Maybe I'd better just crawl, instead."

"No, really, Kel. There's a slight incline behind the house. I can take you to the top and give you a big push..."

"Jared!" Kelly interrupted Shane's nonsense with a wail. "Can't you do anything with this son of yours?"

Leaning against the arm of his wife's chair, Jared chuckled. "I could take him behind the woodshed, if you like, but it's never done much good before."

Shane snorted. "Like you could get me there now."

Jared lifted an eyebrow and looked at his full-grown son. His tone was very mild when he asked, "You want me to give it a try?"

"Er, no," Shane said, quickly holding up his hands.

"I take it back, Dad. You probably *could* get me there now."

Everyone laughed.

Vinnie looked ruefully at Jared. "I wish my sons had such a healthy fear of me."

"We love you, Pop—you know that," Tony quipped. "But Mom's the one who makes us tremble in our shoes."

"And so you should," petite, gentle-faced Carla D'Alessandro murmured. "I can still send you to a corner if you misbehave, Antonio."

"And he'd still go, if you told him to," Joe said with a grin. "As would Michael and I."

While Tony's children dissolved into giggles at the thought of their father being sent to a corner, and Kevin Samples joked with his own blushing teenage daughter, Joe thought about how much he'd looked forward to having his own children, eventually. It was something he'd always taken for granted, even as he'd been more aware lately of the passage of time. Marriage and children were simply a given in his family, considered the greatest blessings anyone could have in life.

He'd had to do some serious thinking since that momentous telephone conversation with Brynn. And he'd come to the conclusion that, yes, he had seen her—at least subconsciously—as a potential mother of the children he'd expected to have. He was thirty-five, after all; he'd probably subliminally been looking for a mate for the past year or more.

No one had "clicked" until he'd met Brynn. It hadn't taken him long to decide it was Brynn he'd fallen in love with, and not the hypothetical children he could have had with her.

A decision about children could wait. First, he had to

convince Brynn it was okay to smile when he walked into a room.

Kelly seemed to be in no mood to be used as a convenient excuse. She was in no hurry to leave the party being thrown in her honor. She thrived on the solicitous attention after so many weeks in the hospital, and she didn't want to give it up too soon.

But weariness finally claimed her and she agreed to Brynn's suggestion that she should go lie down for a while. There was no lack of offers to help them, but Joe stepped forward, grasped the handles of the wheelchair and assured everyone he would take care of everything.

No one attempted to argue with him.

"I have to go, anyway," Shane said, glancing at his watch. "See you, Kelly. And, Brynn—"

Glancing at Joe, he kissed her cheek, a look of sheer devilry in his eyes. "I will most definitely be seeing you later."

Joe was almost growling when he wheeled Kelly out of Michelle's den and through the house to the kitchen door, which led directly to the path to the guest house. He maneuvered the chair skillfully up the single step onto the tiny front porch of the guest house. Brynn opened the door and helped him get Kelly inside.

"I don't know why I'm so tired," Kelly murmured— her first hint of complaint all day. "It's not as if I've really done anything today."

"Cut yourself some slack, Kelly. Even with the physical therapy you've had every day, six weeks in the hospital is debilitating. You'll get your strength back as you get back on your feet."

"I'm ready for that," Kelly said heartily.

Ten minutes later, she was comfortably ensconced in

her bedroom, pillows propped behind her on the bed, her right leg supported, a book, glass of water, a radio and a television remote within her reach. Brynn urged her to call out if she needed anything, and then she and Joe left Kelly to rest.

Joe followed Brynn into the kitchen, where she busied herself making a pot of coffee she didn't want. At least it gave her something to do with her hands, and someplace to look other than Joe.

"You're being very quiet," he commented, leaning against the counter, watching her every movement. "Are you mad at me?"

"I'm annoyed," she replied, trying to keep her voice cool. "Why did you make such a production of—of kissing me in front of everyone? Now they're all going to think you and I are...involved."

"You and I *are* involved," he answered, his tone no warmer than her own. "Seriously involved, as far as I'm concerned."

She swallowed. "Still, I think I should have had a say in when—or if—we decided to go public with it."

"All I did was kiss you. I hardly made a general announcement that we've been to bed together. Twice."

Her cheeks heated. "You didn't have to announce it. Now they're probably all wondering."

"These qualms didn't seem to occur to you while you were plastered all over Shane in front of everyone."

Brynn's jaw dropped. If she didn't know better, she would swear that Joe D'Alessandro was jealous of Shane. Jealous—over her!

"Everyone knows that Shane and I are just friends," she retorted pointedly. Cousins, maybe, she could have added, but she wasn't ready to talk about that until she had heard from Ryan.

"And everyone probably suspects now that you and I are more than just friends," Joe shot back. "I'm not interested in an illicit affair with you, Brynn. You aren't my mistress, and I refuse to treat you as such. Either we're on or we're off, but I won't have any more of this in-between."

She raised both eyebrows, turned slowly toward him, and planted her fists on her hips. "Excuse me? You won't have it? You're setting the rules now?"

He threw his hands up in exasperation. "We don't *have* rules. This isn't a game, Brynn. I love you, damn it."

She started to snap back at him...and then his words sank in.

She sagged against the counter, the coffee scoop tumbling from her suddenly limp hand to the floor. If there *had* been rules to their relationship, Joe had just changed them drastically.

It took her a moment to recover enough to speak. "I don't—"

"You heard what I said. And maybe now you understand why I don't want to sneak around to see you when there's no one around to know. Why I don't like watching you smiling at another man and trying to pretend I'm not in the room."

Brynn spread her hands. "Joe, there is nothing going on between Shane and me. There will never be anything between us."

He sighed and ran a hand through his hair. "I know that," he admitted after a brief pause. "I'm sorry, Brynn. I was out of line to make comments about Shane. He's a nice guy, and I understand why you like him. I just can't help envying him because you are so comfortable with him."

She wanted to tell him that she was comfortable with Shane because she didn't have to worry about hurting Shane. About being hurt by him. But she didn't know how to say the words. She bit her lip, instead.

Joe reached out to touch her face, his fingers lingering to cup her cheek. "I promised you I would be patient, didn't I? I haven't done a very good job of that, I'm afraid. Being patient isn't easy for a D'Alessandro. But I'll try."

"Joe...about what I told you on the telephone the other night..."

"I heard every word you said," he assured her. "But nothing I heard made any difference in the way I feel about you. I love you."

She closed her eyes, letting the words echo in her head, wanting desperately to believe them, yet terrified that she might actually start to do so. "Sometimes," she murmured, forcing herself to look at him, "loving each other isn't enough. Sometimes the differences between two people are just too big to overcome."

"Tell that to either of my brothers—Tony and Michelle, or Michael and his wife, Joy—who, by the way, is Asian American. To my parents, for that matter, who have little more in common than their Italian heritage and their love for each other and their family. Try telling Jared Walker and his bubbly, impulsive, demonstrative wife, Cassie, that they are too different to make a life together."

He reached out and took her hands, gripping them, pulling her close to him. "From what I've seen, when two people love each other, there's nothing they can't overcome together. *Do* we love each other, Brynn?"

"There's something I have to tell you. About my father..."

"I want to hear it," he assured her. "Later. First, answer my question."

"It's important, Joe. My father..."

"Was a teenage alcoholic. You've already told me. Do you love me, Brynn?"

His mouth was only an inch above hers now, his eyes locked with her own. He had to see the truth there, so there was really no point in denying it further. "Yes. But..."

His mouth covered hers before she could finish the caveat.

Brynn's hands settled on his shoulders, clutching the fabric of his shirt. She closed her eyes and opened to him, unable to resist him while his words of love still resonated in her mind.

It didn't matter that Kelly was resting in the other room. That a dozen Walkers and D'Alessandros were milling in the house next door, probably speculating about Joe and Brynn. That there were still so many unanswered questions ahead of them. She loved him. He said he loved her.

For just this moment, Brynn allowed herself to be purely happy.

Joe groaned deep in his chest and hauled her closer, crushing her against him. The countertop was hard against her back when he pressed her against it, his hands going to the hem of her top and under. His palms were warm against her back, hot against her breasts. She gasped and crowded closer to him, reveling in the evidence of his desire for her.

"Ancora," Joe murmured into her mouth. "Tell me again."

"I love you, Joe. I..."

Her words were muffled by a kiss that nearly melted

her knees. She was trembling from head to toe when he finally lifted his head.

"So, will you marry me?"

A blast of ice water couldn't have cooled Brynn down any faster. She jerked herself out of Joe's arms. "*What* did you say?"

He made a face. "Too much, too soon?"

"I would say so. Joe, we haven't even been on a real date. We can't even talk yet about getting m-m…"

"Married," he supplied for her.

She gulped. "Stop saying that."

Joe lifted her left hand to his lips and nibbled a kiss on her knuckles. "Am I making you nervous, *cara?*"

"Yes."

"Good." He sounded so smug—as if he knew it was just a matter of time until he wheedled the answer he wanted from her.

"Joe…"

He touched the tip of his tongue to her ring finger. "I'll try to be patient, Brynn. But you know how D'Alessandros are when it comes to patience."

She'd just gotten accustomed to the idea of dating him publicly. But marriage—she wasn't nearly ready to consider that.

"What about Leonardo?" she blurted.

That made him lift his head. "Who?" he asked blankly.

Her cheeks went crimson. "You know…your great-aunt Luisa…the son she wants you to name after her father."

Joe shook his head in exasperation. "Brynn, I *love* you. I want you to be my wife. Whatever we decide about children, we'll make the decision that's right for us. Not my aunt. Not my family. Not anyone else. Just us.''

He was so good at countering her arguments. Making her believe she mattered to him more than anything else. No one, except maybe Kelly, had ever made her feel that way before.

No one except Kelly had ever truly loved her before.

It was an incredibly seductive feeling. It almost made her believe that anything was possible.

''I...''

Whatever she might have said was interrupted by the chime of her doorbell. Brynn took advantage of the escape and hurried into the living room to answer the door.

Her heart, which had been racing from the encounter with Joe, nearly stopped when she identified her caller.

Ryan Walker was standing on her doorstep, a thick envelope in his hand. ''Hello, Brynn. I have some news for you.''

''I can't believe this.'' It must have been the dozenth time Brynn had spoken those words in the twenty minutes since Ryan had confirmed that the young man Brynn's mother had known as Danny Smith had indeed been Miles Daniel Walker. Ryan had even found a couple more photos of Miles and Connie Larkin cuddled together only days before the car accident, and a police report listing Connie as the sole survivor of the accident that had killed her boyfriend and two other young men.

The evidence was strong that Brynn was Miles's daughter.

''I'm as certain as I can be without DNA testing— and we'll arrange for that, if it will ease your mind. It isn't necessary as far as I'm concerned.'' Ryan smiled at her. "I'm completely ready to claim you as my niece."

"Wow, Brynn. You have uncles." Sitting in her wheelchair—having been awakened by the doorbell—Kelly looked almost as stunned as Brynn felt. "Aunts. And cousins."

"Layla's going to cry," Joe predicted wryly. He sat next to Brynn on the couch, and he'd said little as Ryan had produced his evidence, after first asking Brynn if she minded onlookers. Brynn had insisted that Joe and Kelly stay for the news. She still wasn't sure how Joe actually felt about the stunning revelation.

Ryan's firm mouth slanted upward. "Layla always cries. That's how we know when she's happy."

"When are you going to tell everyone, Brynn?" Kelly asked eagerly.

"I...don't know." The very thought made her knees weak.

"Why not now?" Ryan suggested. "Joe and Lauren and Taylor are at Michelle's with the others, so all your aunts and uncles are gathered there except Lindsay and Grant. They've decided to order a truckload of pizzas—you know how they seize every opportunity to have a family party. This would be a great time."

"I'm not sure I can tell them," Brynn murmured, glancing instinctively at Joe. "What if they don't believe me? What if they think I'm trying to con them or something? What if...?"

"They'll believe Ryan," Joe assured her. "And no one is going to think you're trying to con them, Brynn. Give them more credit than that."

"They'll be delighted," Ryan agreed. "Surely you've noticed that this family operates on the philosophy that there's always room for more."

Brynn swallowed, then stood and nodded. She supposed there would be no benefit to putting this off. "All right," she said, looking a bit shyly at her uncle. "Let's go tell them."

Chapter Fifteen

Kelly had no intention of being left out of the grand announcement, of course. Joe wheeled her back to the main house, with Ryan hovering nearby if he needed assistance.

The spacious den was even more crowded now than it had been before, but there was still room for a few more. Joe parked Kelly's chair in a convenient spot, where they watched as Ryan cleared his throat and signaled for everyone's attention.

"Brynn and I have something we want to tell you," he said, pulling Brynn to his side when she showed a tendency to want to hide behind him.

From Taylor's smile, Joe assumed Ryan had already broken the news to his wife. Everyone else looked curious about what news Ryan shared with Tony and Michelle's nanny.

Brynn looked at Ryan, obviously pleading for him to be the one to speak.

He nodded. "It's about Miles," he began, looking at Layla.

Layla, who'd been the primary caretaker for her younger siblings until they'd been separated when she was only ten, pressed a hand to her chest. "Miles? Our brother?"

Ryan nodded. "Yes. He..."

"Is he still alive?" Layla asked, leaping to a hopeful conclusion. "Were the reports of his death incorrect?"

"No, Layla," Ryan answered gently. "Miles really did die in that car accident on his eighteenth birthday. What we didn't know was that he wasn't using his legal name at the time. He'd been introducing himself as Danny Smith—I really don't know why, unless it was just to separate himself from his past, the way Joe and I did when we were teenagers."

Tony frowned. "I never found that name in my research. Only a death certificate in the name of Miles Daniel Walker."

"Which was still his legal name," Ryan agreed. "But not the one he was using with his friends—or his girlfriend, Connie Larkin."

"Larkin?" Michelle repeated, looking quickly at Brynn.

"Brynn's mother," Ryan elaborated. "She was actually in the accident with Miles. Connie was the only survivor."

"What a strange coincidence." Ryan's sister-in-law, Lauren Walker, shook her head in amazement. "Brynn's mother knew your brother."

"I think there's a bit more to the coincidence than that," her husband murmured, studying his twin's face.

"Yes." Ryan cleared his throat. "Brynn was born less than seven months after that accident."

The room went very still. Joe watched as Layla's face suddenly drained of color. "Are you saying…?"

"Connie Larkin told Brynn that a boy named Danny Smith was her father. She said she was unknowingly pregnant by him the night of the accident. I have photographs of Connie and Miles together, looking very cozy."

"Oh, my God." Michelle covered her cheeks with her hands. "I hired my *niece?*"

Brynn spoke for the first time then, looking anxiously earnest. "I didn't know, either. I swear, I had no idea. Shane was visiting me Monday evening and he saw a photograph of my parents. I told him how my father died, and he put all the clues together. He went to Ryan with his suspicions, and Ryan asked my permission to investigate."

"Brynn didn't know," Ryan collaborated. "She was as stunned as the rest of us. She even volunteered to take a blood test. But I think we've already found the truth."

Jared looked closely at his brother. "You really believe Brynn is Miles's daughter?"

"Yeah. I really do. Stranger coincidences have happened," Ryan added, smiling crookedly at his wife.

Apparently satisfied with Ryan's certainty, Jared stepped in front of Brynn. "Welcome to the family, Brynn," he said, and pressed a gentle kiss on her cheek.

Layla burst into tears.

Mass pandemonium reigned for the next several minutes. Joe and Kelly stayed back out of the way as Brynn was mobbed by her newly discovered family. Tony and Michelle and their children—who didn't quite understand what was going on but knew it was something nice. Layla, Kevin and Brittany. Jared, Cassie and Molly. Joe and Lauren Walker and young Casey. Ryan and Taylor and their twins.

Even Vinnie and Carla heartily welcomed Brynn to the Walker family, teasingly referring to her as their "niece-in-law."

Joe glanced down at Kelly, catching a fleetingly wistful look on her face that might have been tinged with anxiety. He understood both emotions.

He couldn't quite define his own feelings about the revelation that Brynn was a member of the Walker clan. While he knew he should be delighted that she'd been brought together with her family, he was aware of a selfish reluctance to share her with them.

He'd become more possessive of Brynn than he'd realized, apparently. Now all these other people had an emotional claim to her. And there was a part of him that didn't like it.

He was a jerk.

Kelly was probably feeling much the same way, he thought. He laid a hand on her shoulder. "Brynn will always think of you as her sister," he murmured.

Kelly smiled up at him. "I know. I'm thrilled for Brynn, really. She has always wanted a family so desperately, no matter how often she tried to deny it. Now she has a big one."

Joe nodded. He, too, was pleased that Brynn had found her family...but he still wanted to make her a part of his own. She had said she loved him. He wouldn't give up now until she was legally a D'Alessandro, as well as a Walker.

Later that evening, Brynn sat next to Layla Samples on one of the comfortable sofas in Michelle's den. Her

hand was held snugly in Layla's, who had hardly let go
of Brynn since the grand announcement. The other
adults were gathered around them, while Brittany su-
pervised the younger children in another room.

"We've learned so little about Miles's life after we
were separated," Layla said with a sigh. "I had so
hoped he was happy."

"From what my mother told me, he was always
laughing and joking," Brynn offered hesitantly. "He
was impulsive and mischievous—which often got him
into trouble—and my mother was afraid he had a drinking problem, but she seemed to believe he was happy.
Especially when they were together..."

"A drinking problem." Layla grimaced. "Poor Miles
must have inherited our father's weakness for alcohol."

Brynn bit her lip and glanced at Joe, who'd said so
little during the evening. She wondered what Layla
would say if she knew how many flaws had come from
Brynn's mother's side. What would the D'Alessandros
think if they knew their youngest son wanted to marry
the daughter of an alcoholic and a manic-depressive?

Michelle nodded, looking pensive. "I worried about
that before Tony and I had children," she confessed.
"We decided to make it very clear to them that a tendency toward alcoholism runs in their family, and that
they must always be very careful. We want them to
understand that they have the power to choose whether
to start down that path or not."

"You have Joe and Ryan's pretty, pale-blue eyes.
And your father's smile," Layla murmured, still looking at Brynn. "Why didn't I see that before?"

"You weren't looking," Ryan suggested.

"I'm so glad we found you." Layla patted Brynn's

hand with both of hers. "Mother and Miles brought you to us—I just know they did. I feel it."

"You don't really think our mother's spirit caused a terrible car accident, Layla," Joe Walker objected.

She was undaunted by his cynicism. "Of course not. But she could have arranged for Joe and Michael to be there when it happened. And for Tony and Michelle to need a nanny at just the right time. And for Shane to see that photograph…"

Several of the others were laughing by the time she'd finished postulating, though their laughter was good-natured and affectionate.

Brynn glanced across the room at Kelly, who was talking quietly with Taylor and Ryan. Kelly looked tired, Brynn thought. And she herself was suddenly exhausted. So much had happened that day—almost too much for her to take in all at once.

"We'd better go," she said, gently disentangling her hand from Layla's. "Kelly needs to rest."

"Yes, of course she does. We've neglected her terribly tonight, haven't we?" Layla asked penitently. "We'll talk more later, Brynn."

Brynn nodded and stood. "Kelly? Ready to go?"

"I'll help you," Joe said quickly, taking hold of the wheelchair before anyone else could offer. No one attempted to argue with him.

Brynn said good-night to everyone, accepted what seemed liked dozens of kisses on the cheek and finally made her escape with Joe and Kelly.

She was experiencing "family overload," she decided. To go so abruptly from being alone to being a part of such a large group was a staggering experience. Almost overwhelming.

And now she had to deal with Joe.

* * *

Joe made sure Kelly was safely inside the guest house, then turned to Brynn. "I know you'll need to help Kelly get ready for bed, so I won't stay."

"Walk Joe out to his car, Brynn," Kelly ordered, her green eyes twinkling with mischief. "You can't give him a proper good-night kiss with me here to watch."

Brynn blushed. And then glared at Kelly. "I'm sure Joe can find his way to his car without me."

"Kelly's right," Joe said, catching Brynn's hand and pulling her toward the front door. "You should walk me out. I'm really looking forward to that proper good-night kiss."

Brynn was still sputtering protests when he towed her outside. She heard Kelly laughing behind them.

"I really can't stay out long," she said when Joe closed the door, leaving them out in the warm summer night. "Kelly's tired, and she can't get ready for bed without help."

"Are you going to be able to manage? It'll be a couple of weeks before she's getting around on her own. She'll need a lot of help."

"I can manage. She'll be fine once I've got her into her chair each morning. I can check on her several times during the day. Michelle's already offered to hire help, if we need it, though I hate for her to have to pay for both a nanny and a part-time nurse."

"Don't worry about that. Michelle can afford whatever help she needs. And you're family now."

There was that word again. Family. Brynn cleared her throat. "Anyway, I'm going to be very busy for the next few weeks, between taking care of Kelly and the children. I can't neglect my responsibilities to any of them."

"I get your hint, Brynn. You're asking me to give you time and space. I promised to try to be patient, and I will. But don't ask me to stay away completely. That's more than I can give."

And more than she could ask, Brynn thought. She didn't want Joe to stay away completely...whatever her fears regarding him.

They reached his car and Joe turned to take her into his arms. "About that good-night kiss..."

He bent his head to cover her mouth with his. Brynn responded as she always did when Joe kissed her... with all her heart.

"One day," he murmured a short while later, "your home will be with me. I won't have to leave you at the end of the evening. But in the meantime, remember that I love you. That I will always love you, no matter how many more surprises lie ahead for us."

"I love you, too," she whispered, unable to hold the words inside. "But I can't talk about the future tonight. Too much has happened today."

"I understand. Or at least, I'm trying to. Good night, *cara*."

He climbed into his car and started the engine. Brynn watched him as he drove away.

They both knew he would be back very soon—and that his patience was limited.

Joe's patience lasted exactly two more weeks. He and Brynn had hardly seen each other during that time, between Brynn's responsibilities and his own demanding career. Brynn knew he was growing frustrated with her, and she desperately missed being with him, but she needed that time apart from him to do a great deal of

thinking about where their relationship was going—
where she wanted it to go.

She still hadn't reached any solid conclusions when
he basically kidnapped her one Friday evening.

She had just left the children with their parents and
had walked back into her own house to make dinner for
Kelly. The smell of food—barbecue, she thought—hit
her as soon as she entered the door. She blinked in
surprise. Kelly was getting around amazingly well, but
Brynn hadn't thought her capable of preparing a meal
yet.

Shane Walker appeared in the kitchen doorway. "Hi,
Brynn. Don't worry about cooking tonight. I brought
barbecue for two. Kelly and I are going to chow down
and then play Scrabble or something for a couple of
hours."

"You brought barbecue for two?" Brynn repeated,
noting that she'd been excluded from his evening plans.
"Er…"

Joe D'Alessandro stepped into the doorway behind
Shane. His smile dared her to cause him any trouble.
"You and I," he said smoothly, "are going out for
dinner."

"We are?" Brynn placed her hands on her hips.
"Funny, I don't remember being asked if I wanted to
go out to dinner."

"Just shut up and go, Brynn," Kelly called from the
kitchen, her voice rich with laughter. "You need some
time off, and we knew you wouldn't take it unless you
were forced to. So, we're not giving you any choice.
Go out and relax, let someone cook for you for a
change."

Brynn was still arguing when Joe hustled her out the
door and into his car.

"You're very pleased with yourself, aren't you?" she asked him as he drove away from the estate, looking rather smug.

"A bit," he admitted shamelessly. "I thought it was very clever of me to arrange this with Kelly and Shane without you finding out."

"You should have asked me, Joe."

"I wanted it to be a surprise."

"And if I hadn't wanted to come with you?"

He shrugged. "Then you wouldn't have. I didn't twist your arm behind your back, Brynn."

She settled back into her seat, knowing he was right. If she'd been adamantly opposed to coming with him, she would have stuck to her refusal, and there would have been little he could have done about it.

Joe glanced over at her. "Want me to take you back home?"

She sighed. "No. Just don't get into the habit of planning my evenings for me, will you?"

He nodded. "Shane seemed pleased to have an excuse to spend the evening with Kelly. They've become good friends during the past few weeks, I think."

"Yes. He made a point of visiting her in the hospital several times. Shane's adopted her as another cousin, I think. They seem to have become great pals."

"I can understand why. Kelly's very special. I've grown quite fond of her myself. I'll enjoy having her for my honorary sister-in-law."

"Joe..." Brynn looked at him warningly. "We weren't going to talk about things like that yet, remember?"

"You said we couldn't get married because we hadn't had a real date," he reminded her. "I'm counting tonight as a date. Which means we can start planning the wedding tomorrow.''

"You,'' she told him with an exhale of exasperation, "are impossible.''

"Nothing, for us, is impossible, Brynn. I'm waiting as patiently as I can for you to figure that out.''

"That isn't what I meant.''

His smile was warm. "I know.''

She had expected him to take her to a restaurant. He took her to an upscale apartment building, instead. "Is, um, this where you live?'' she asked as he pulled into a parking space.

"Yes. We're dining in tonight.''

"You're cooking?''

He opened his door. "Let's just say I'm providing the meal.''

Somewhat nervously, she allowed him to escort her into the elevator.

Joe's apartment was lovely, if a bit sparsely furnished. As Brynn admired the view from the glass wall of his living room, he explained that he'd only lived there a year and hadn't really had time to decorate yet, since he spent so many hours at work every day.

And then he led her into the dining room, where a beautifully appointed table set for two awaited them. Brynn gasped at the sight of flowers and candles, china, crystal and silver. This room, too, had a glass wall that overlooked the Dallas skyline, the perfect sunset adding just the right backdrop for the setting. "Joe. This is beautiful!''

He nodded in satisfaction. "Looks good, doesn't it?''

"How…?''

"My cousin Anne Marie's a caterer,'' he confessed.

"I called her and asked her to have this waiting for us. The meal is in the kitchen, ready to be eaten."

Joe lit the candles on the table, flipped a switch that caused soft, romantic music to waft through the room and then held Brynn's chair for her. "Sit down," he urged. "Let me serve you tonight."

Almost unbearably touched, she took her seat.

The meal was exquisite, not that she was fully aware of what she was eating. No one had ever done anything like this for her before. She was so bedazzled she did well to remember how to hold her fork.

They were having tiramisu for dessert when she finally recovered enough to ask, "Is this something you do often?"

Watching her from across the table, Joe shook his head with a faint smile. "I've never done this before. To be honest, I'm amazed it all worked out."

"It's the sweetest thing anyone has ever done for me," she told him candidly. "Thank you."

"I wanted our first real date to be special. I love you, Brynn."

She swallowed and set her fork on her plate. "It still makes me nervous to hear you say that," she confessed.

"Why?"

"We've known each other such a short time, really. Less than three months. I'm afraid you don't really know me at all. That you've somehow gotten an impression of me that's different from the way I really am."

He shook his head. "Would you like me to list everything I know about you? Everything I love about you? Your courage. Your kindness. Your intelligence. Your resilience. Your humor. Your shyness. The passion you keep so well hidden... until we make love and you open yourself to it. You're everything I've ever wanted, Brynn. I'm not going to change my mind about that, no matter how much longer we wait.''

She blinked back a film of tears. ''I don't know how you can talk about my courage when I feel like such a coward.''

''Because I know the reason for your fears, and I understand them,'' he assured her. ''But I believe you and I can overcome whatever obstacles might lie ahead of us. Layla believes a benevolent destiny brought you back into her family. Maybe she's right. I feel the same way about whatever force brought us together that day on the highway. We were meant to be together. And whatever it takes, I won't give up until you accept that, too.''

Brynn drew a deep, unsteady breath. ''I think I've loved you since the moment I opened my eyes after the accident and found you leaning over me, asking if I was all right. Maybe it was destiny—or maybe nothing more than coincidence. But I'm ready to admit that we do belong together, Joe. I love you.''

''Marry me.'' His tone had grown urgent now, his dark eyes hot.

One tear spilled down her cheek. ''Yes.''

His chair teetered precariously as he shoved it back from the table. A moment later, he was at her side, hauling her to her feet and into his arms.

Brynn wrapped her arms around his neck and lost herself in his kiss.

They didn't bother clearing the dishes before they left the dining room.

''There are still so many things we have to settle,'' Brynn murmured a long time later, her voice still husky.

Lying on his back, his eyes closed, his damp hair tousled, Joe tightened his arm around her bare shoulders and grunted. "We'll talk about them later."

"We can't wait too long. It still worries me...my background, I mean. I had so many strikes against me."

"And you turned out beautifully," he murmured, pressing a kiss to her forehead. "You aren't mentally unstable, like your mother or her mother. You aren't an alcoholic, like your father or his father. There's no reason to believe your children, if you decide to have any, will inherit those traits, either."

She sighed faintly. "I have so much baggage from my childhood, Joe. I won't always be an easy person to live with, I'm afraid."

"Everyone has baggage from the past, *cara*. We simply have to learn to stow it in a dark closet somewhere and leave it alone. Fortunately, you've come into a family that knows all about childhood scars. Any one of your aunts or uncles would happily talk to you about how they overcame their pasts."

"I want to get my degree. I want to teach."

"And you will. In fact, you should register as a full-time student this fall. There's no need for you to work while you take classes. I make enough to support us both."

She frowned. "I'm accustomed to supporting myself."

He chuckled and kissed her again. "Damn, you're independent. I love that about you, too, but sometimes it can be a pain in the neck. Let me help you with your education, Brynn. Please."

"We'll discuss it," she conceded. "But what about Michelle? I would be leaving her without a nanny again."

''She'll find someone else. Whether you're working for her or not, you will always be her niece and the children's cousin—her sister-in-law and the children's aunt, after you and I are married. You will always be a very special member of both families.''

''I love you, Joe.''

''*Anch'io ti amo, tesoro.* I love you, too. Forever.''

''Forever'' was not a word that had been an integral part of Brynn's vocabulary in the past. That had changed the day Joe D'Alessandro had entered her life, claiming the heart she'd always protected so carefully.

Love finds even the hidden heart.

Remembering the fortune cookie message, she smiled against Joe's shoulder and thought about destiny.

She was beginning to believe in it after all.

* * * * *

Watch for Shane's story,
THAT FIRST SPECIAL KISS,
coming in September from Gina Wilkins
and Silhouette Special Edition.

Silhouette ® SPECIAL EDITION ®

Don't miss these heartwarming love stories coming to Silhouette Special Edition!

June '99 BABY LOVE by Victoria Pade (#1249)
A Ranching Family Ry McDermot was capable of caring for his ranch, but was at a loss when it came to his orphaned nephew. Until nurse Tallie Shanahan stepped in to give him lessons on baby love....

Aug. '99 I NOW PRONOUNCE YOU MOM & DAD by Diana Whitney (#1261)
For the Children Lydia Farnsworth would have been happy never to see former flame Powell Greer again. So why was she marrying him? For their godchildren, of course! And maybe for herself...?

Oct. '99 SURPRISE DELIVERY by Susan Mallery (#1273)
Heather Fitzpatrick became irresistibly drawn to the pilot who unexpectedly delivered her precious baby. Now if only she could get her heart—and her gorgeous hero—out of the clouds...!

THAT'S MY BABY!
Sometimes bringing up baby can bring surprises... and showers of love.

Available at your favorite retail outlet.

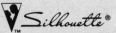

Silhouette® SPECIAL EDITION®

presents **THE BRIDAL CIRCLE,** a brand-new miniseries honoring friendship, family and love...

THE BRIDAL CIRCLE

by

Andrea Edwards

They dreamed of marrying and leaving their small town behind—but soon discovered there's no place like home for true love!

IF I ONLY HAD A...HUSBAND (May '99)

Penny Donnelly had tried desperately to forget charming millionaire Brad Corrigan. But her heart had a memory—and a will—of its own. And Penny's heart was set on Brad becoming her husband....

SECRET AGENT GROOM (August '99)

When shy-but-sexy Heather Mahoney bumbles onto secret agent Alex Waterstone's undercover mission, the only way to protect the innocent beauty is to claim her as his lady love. Will Heather carry out her own secret agenda and claim Alex as her groom?

PREGNANT & PRACTICALLY MARRIED
(November '99)

Pregnant Karin Spencer had suddenly lost her memory and *gained* a pretend fiancé. Though their match was make-believe, Jed McCarron was her dream man. Could this bronco-bustin' cowboy give up his rodeo days for family ways?

Available at your favorite retail outlet.

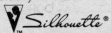
Silhouette®

Silhouette SPECIAL EDITION®

That SPECIAL *Woman!*

She's a wife, mother—she's you! And beside each Special Edition woman stands a wonderfully special man! Don't miss these upcoming titles only from Silhouette Special Edition!

❤❤❤

May 1999 HER VERY OWN FAMILY
by Gina Wilkins (SE #1243)
Family Found: Sons & Daughters

All her life, Brynn Larkin had yearned for a home—and a wonderful husband. So when sexy surgeon Joe D'Allesandro offered Brynn a helping hand—and made her an honorary member of his loving clan—had she finally found her very own family?

❤❤❤

July 1999 HUNTER'S WOMAN
by Lindsay McKenna (SE #1255)
Morgan's Mercenaries: The Hunters

Catt Alborak was ready for battle when she was thrown back together with Ty Hunter, the mesmerizing mercenary from her past. As much as the headstrong lady doc tried to resist her fierce protector, their fiery passion knew no bounds!

❤❤❤

September 1999 THEIR OTHER MOTHER
by Janis Reams Hudson (SE #1267)
Wilders of Wyatt County

Sparks flew when widowed rancher Ace Wilder reluctantly let Belinda Randall care for his three sons. Would the smitten duo surrender to their undeniable attraction—and embark on a blissful future together?

Look for *That Special Woman!* every other month from some of your favorite authors!
Available at your favorite retail outlet.

♥ *Silhouette*®

SSETSW

Coming in May 1999

BABY *Fever*

by
New York Times Bestselling Author

KASEY MICHAELS

When three sisters hear their biological
clocks ticking, they know it's
time for action.

But who will they get to father their babies?

**Find out how the road to motherhood
leads to love in this brand-new collection.**

Available at your favorite retail outlet.

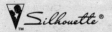
Silhouette®

THE MACGREGORS OF OLD...

#1 *New York Times* bestselling author

NORA ROBERTS

has won readers' hearts with her enormously popular MacGregor family saga. Now read about the MacGregors proud and passionate Scottish forebears in this romantic, tempestuous tale set against the bloody background of the historic battle of Culloden.

Coming in July 1999

REBELLION

One look at the ravishing red-haired beauty and Brigham Langston was captivated. But though Serena MacGregor had the face of an angel, she was a wildcat who spurned his advances with a rapier-sharp tongue. To hot-tempered Serena, Brigham was just another Englishman to be despised. But in the arms of the dashing and dangerous English lord, the proud Scottish beauty felt her hatred melting with the heat of their passion.

Available at your favorite retail outlet.

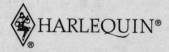

HARLEQUIN®